Material Modernisms

Series Editors
Faye Hammill
University of Glasgow
Glasgow, UK

Celia Marshik
Stony Brook University
Stony Brook, USA

Andrew Thacker
Nottingham Trent University
Nottingham, UK

This series brings together studies that focus on modern literature and its relationship to, among other topics, contemporary print culture, technology, media, fashion, art and design, and of course, objects and material culture. Whether scholars work on fashion, food, modes of transport, paper ephemera, or other types of objects and materials, they are united in arguing that writers not only imbued their works with references to the physical world but also thought out major questions of politics, ethics, and philosophy through things. The definition of modernism is expansive, extending into what is often known as 'late modernism' (into the second half of the twentieth century), popular culture, and the institutions of middlebrow culture. Though the series is based in literary studies, it welcomes interdisciplinary approaches that connect literature to other disciplines, such as art and design history, music, architecture, cultural studies, anthropology, or digital humanities.

Maud Ellmann

The Vacuum Cleaner

A Cultural Investigation

Maud Ellmann
Cambridge, UK

ISSN 2661-8273   ISSN 2661-8281   (electronic)
Material Modernisms
ISBN 978-3-031-56665-3   ISBN 978-3-031-56666-0   (eBook)
https://doi.org/10.1007/978-3-031-56666-0

Cover illustration: Pattern © Melisa Hasan

This Palgrave Macmillan imprint is published by the registered company Springer Nature Switzerland AG.
The registered company address is: Gewerbestrasse 11, 6330 Cham, Switzerland

Paper in this product is recyclable.

In memory of Stephen Ellmann

ACKNOWLEDGEMENTS

First and foremost, I thank Randy L. Berlin and the late Melvin R. Berlin for endowing the professorship I held at the University of Chicago from 2010 to 2023 and for their kindness to me throughout those exciting and rewarding years. The Visiting Committee of the Humanities Division of the University also provided generous support for my work. I'm especially indebted to Zachary Hope for his resourcefulness and efficiency in tracking down the permissions for the images in this book: a complex and time-consuming task. The Humanities Division under the leadership of Dean Anne W. Robertson provided a much-appreciated subvention for the cost of permissions. In addition, I thank the National Humanities Center for the M.H. Abrams Fellowship that enabled me to get started on this project. The Center's librarians went the extra mile to help me track down obscure publications about vacuum cleaners and traveling salesmen. I'm also deeply grateful to Anita Sokolsky for her careful reading and astute criticism, as well as to Frances Ferguson, David Hillman, Josephine McDonagh, Adelais Mills, Ann Reynolds, and Nicholas Royle for their constructive and imaginative suggestions. My husband, John Wilkinson, patiently read draft after draft and was always perceptive and encouraging. Paul Willetts kindly provided me with a copy of the (miraculously) rediscovered manuscript of Julian Maclaren-Ross's "vacuum cleaner novel" *Of Love and Hunger*, or as it was formerly titled *The Salesman Only Rings Once*. Finally, I thank my late brother Steve Ellmann, to whom this book is dedicated in memoriam, for reminding me that the unlikely spy in Graham Greene's *Our Man in Havana* is a vacuum cleaner salesman.

Contents

LIST OF FIGURES

CHAPTER 1

Introduction

Abstract The iconic appliance of the twentieth-century domestic revolution, the vacuum cleaner has gradually evolved from a luxury gimmick into a household necessity. Beginning with a close reading of Raymond Carver's story "Collectors," which involves an unexpected visit from a vacuum cleaner salesman, this introduction outlines the cultural repercussions of this appliance in literature and film, including such works as Anna Sebastian's World War II novel *The Monster*, in which the vacuum cleaner and its salesman come to stand for Hitler's tyranny. In common with other domestic appliances, the vacuum cleaner has been largely overlooked by historians of technology who tend to focus on makers (usually male) rather than users (usually female). Vacuum cleaner lore, by contrast, is dominated by a kind of primal scene in which two social actors, the housewife and the door-to-door salesman, confront each other at the threshold of the private home.

Keywords Raymond Carver • Walter Benjamin • Anna Sebastian • History of technology • Door-to-door salesman • Housewife

The traditional witch went to the witches' sabbath riding through the air on a broomstick. The modern witch will go on a vacuum cleaner.
—Sylvia Townsend Warner, "Modern Witches"[1]

© The Author(s), under exclusive license to Springer Nature Switzerland AG 2024
M. Ellmann, *The Vacuum Cleaner*, Material Modernisms,
https://doi.org/10.1007/978-3-031-56666-0_1

1

FLAKES

In Raymond Carver's story "Collectors" (1975), the nameless narrator, "out of work" and possibly on the run, is startled by an unexpected visit from a vacuum cleaner salesman.[2] This "old guy, fat and bulky under his raincoat" (pp. 102–3), introduces himself as Aubrey Bell—the surname emphasizing his intrusive summons—and explains that Mrs. Slater has won a free vacuuming and carpet shampoo.[3] "Mrs. Slater doesn't live here," the narrator replies (pp. 102, 103). Undeterred, Bell assembles his machine and sets to vacuuming the "twelve-by-fifteen cotton carpet with no-skid backing from Rug City" (p. 108). But Bell's sales pitch scarcely conforms to the stereotype of the door-to-door salesman: peppered with allusions to Auden, Rilke, and Voltaire, this patter verges on the metaphysical. "Every day, every night of our lives, we're leaving little bits of ourselves, flakes of this and that, behind. ... You would be surprised how much of us gets lost, how much of us gathers ... over the years" (pp. 105–6).

Ironically, these "bits of ourselves" seem to have been vacuumed out of the story itself, leaving little trace of the identity of the protagonists. Mrs. Slater, who "doesn't live here," never shows up, and the narrator appears to be in transit, waiting for a message from "up north" (p. 102): "I'm going to be leaving here soon" (p. 110). Nor is the deictic "here" pinned down to a location: the setting is as indeterminate as the characters. "No more explanations" (p. 108): this untagged sentence-fragment applies not only to the salesman but to the narrative itself, which dispenses with any backstory that might explain the narrator's nervousness ("You can't be too careful if you're out of work" [p. 102]) or the salesman's lunatic persistence ("I think I'm losing my mind," says Bell [p. 104]). At the end of the story an envelope posted through the mail slot drops face down onto the carpet. Bell picks it up, intercepting the narrator and, after reading the address—"It's for a Mr. Slater" (p. 109)—promptly pockets the letter. Puzzled rather than indignant, the narrator remarks, "It just seems strange" (p. 110).

Much is strange about this story, especially its dearth of explanatory detail. The vacuum cleaner provides an apt metaphor for Carver's narrative technique, in which the coordinates of time and place, along with the identity of the narrator, are emptied out.[4] Compact and streamlined as today's robovacs, the story dispenses with any cumbrous attachments—names, addresses, flashbacks—that might account for the salesman's

meltdown or the narrator's anxiety. Walter Benjamin argues that the affluent Victorian interior, with its plush upholstery and sumptuous carpets,
was well-adapted to retain the traces of domestic life, traces that detective
fiction developed to decipher.[5] Carver's flakes, by contrast, invite interpretation only to confound it, as if to mock the detective impulse. Instead,
"Collectors" repeatedly disidentifies these traces: Mrs. Slater doesn't live
here, Mr. Slater isn't Mr. Slater, and if the mattress doesn't belong to the
narrator—"It's not my mattress" (p. 106)—neither do the flakes sucked
out of it. Possibly the intrusive salesman alludes to Carver's intrusive editor, Gordon Lish, notorious for the drastic cuts he inflicted on Carver's
stories, emptying them of sentiment and padding. For these elements—
along with date, place, character, and affect—are evacuated from the
narrative.[6]

Oddest of all is the absence of women from this strange meeting of the
door-to-door salesman and his startled "prospect." In vacuum cleaner
lore, this meeting represents a kind of primal scene: a commercial
Annunciation in which the salesman stands in for the angel, surprising the
unwary housewife whose husband, like the biblical Joseph, is conveniently
out of sight.[7] This scene is also primal in that the vacuum cleaner is
designed to suck, which as Ben Watson remarks is "a basic (even primary)
human impulse."[8] But sucking is an impulse associated with maternity,
which makes the absence of women from "Collectors" even more anoma-
lous. Partaking of the homosocial structure of the dirty joke, as Freud
describes it, in which men take advantage of women's absence to indulge
in bawdy repartee at their expense,[9] Carver's male characters connect over
a machine that stands in for the absent housewife, its suction evocative of
breast-feeding and oral sex. What the vacuum cleaner sucks, however, is
not life-giving nourishment but death-laden dust.

This primal scene, as we shall see, recurs throughout vacuum cleaner
fiction—a small but significant canon, which includes Carver, Julian
Maclaren-Ross, Graham Greene, Emily Arnold McCully, C.K. Jaeger,
Sylvia Townsend Warner, and Anna Sebastian, along with some minor
pornographic authors.[10] The present book examines how the vacuum
cleaner figures in literary texts as well as in advertising, the visual arts, and
music. To understand what this appliance signifies in these cultural artefacts requires a multipronged approach, comparable to the strategy Elaine
Freedgood adopts in her study of key objects in the Victorian novel, *The
Ideas in Things*.[11] Freedgood follows Walter Benjamin in distinguishing
between the collector, who elucidates things through "research into their

properties and relations," and the "allegorist"—"the polar opposite of the collector"—who "dislodges things from their context and, from the outset, relies on his profundity to illuminate their meaning." Benjamin admits that these two approaches necessarily impinge on one another: "in every collector hides an allegorist, and in every allegorist a collector."[12] This epigram, incidentally, resonates with Carver's "Collectors," in which the salesman uses the vacuum cleaner to collect the "flakes" of history (like Benjamin's collector) while waxing lyrical about their allegorical significance (like Benjamin's allegorist).

The allegorical impulse has traditionally dominated literary studies, so that objects in novels qualify for critical discussion only when they blossom into metaphor. Freedgood, by contrast, advocates a metonymic inquiry—comparable to Benjamin's collector—which takes the object literally, tracing its contextual relations in a search that extends beyond the covers of the novel itself. This method does not preclude allegory but "delays" it; in any case Freedgood agrees with Gábor Bezeczky that even "the word *literal* is, in most contexts, metaphorical."[13] Yet by holding metaphor at bay, at least provisionally, Freedgood strives to avoid the "routinized literary figuration" by which objects are exalted into symbols, dismissed as decoration, or reduced to what Roland Barthes terms the "reality effect."[14]

Like Freedgood's study, my book draws its object primarily from literature and other media. Of course, the vacuum cleaner represented in these works is incommensurable with the "real thing." But this "thing" is itself a cultural artefact, highly mediated in advance of its representations. And instead of receding into the background, like the mahogany furniture that Freedgood highlights in *Jane Eyre*, the vacuum cleaner looms over its literary frames, threatening to upstage the conventional attractions of plot and character. For this reason, this machine demands to be investigated in its own right, as well as its aesthetic contexts.

The literary texts that inspired this project are two mid-century British novels, Julian MacLaren-Ross's *Of Love and Hunger* (1947) and Graham Greene's *Our Man in Havana* (1958), which are discussed below in Chap. 4. Together these novels span the period from 1939, when *Of Love and Hunger* is set and much of it was written, to the Cold War in the 1950s, which provides the setting for *Our Man in Havana*. During this period the vacuum cleaner slowly gained traction in the British consumer market, evolving from a luxury gimmick into a household necessity, and my study therefore focuses on these mid-century decades. In the mode of the collector, I take the vacuum cleaner literally by exploring its emergence in the commercial arena and its impact on marketing, housework, domestic service, and the peculiarly modern obsession with hygiene. But this machine's literal dimension cannot be unyoked from its fantasia. In fiction and other media, the vacuum cleaner is constantly anthropomorphized; as Marx says of the fetishism of commodities, "the productions of the human brain appear as independent beings endowed with life, and entering into relation both with one another and the human race."[15] The following chapters show how the vacuum cleaner is transformed into multiple "independent beings endowed with life": curmudgeon, windbag, cannibal, dictator, infanticidal mother, freedom fighter, mantrap, and lothario.

Nonetheless—to paraphrase Freud—sometimes a vacuum cleaner is just a vacuum cleaner. My study aims to show how the literal and allegorical dimensions of the vacuum cleaner converge and diverge throughout the history of this appliance. If Carver's "Collectors" invites interpretation as an allegory of editing, for example, Maclaren-Ross's *Of Love and Hunger*, which is based on the author's short-lived career as a vacuum cleaner salesman, exposes the socio-economic context of this commodity while also invoking its mythical penumbra.

The next part of this introduction investigates a range of literary texts and advertising images that demonstrate how the vacuum cleaner is implicated in material, social, and ideological networks. Mid-century advertising promotes the vacuum cleaner as the iconic appliance of the twentieth-century domestic revolution. Representations vary according to cultural context; British ads usually portray the white middle-class housewife as the smiling pilot of the vacuum cleaner, reflecting the decline of domestic service, whereas American ads often place the appliance in the hands of a black "maid," whose labour is lightened by the vacuum cleaner only for the benefit of her white employers. In addition to advertising, the diffusion of vacuum cleaners depended on the door-to-door salesman, whose emergence in mid-century coincided with the rise of the professional housewife.[16] As we shall see, the confrontation of these social actors in what I've designated as the primal scene of vacuum cleaner lore highlights class and gender tensions as well as friction between public and domestic spheres.

RELATIONS STOP NOWHERE

While the vacuum cleaner has come to emblematize mid-century modernity, its origins go back much earlier. The most famous ancestor of today's portable appliance was a horse-drawn cart that makes a cameo appearance in Arnold Bennett's 1923 novel *Riceyman Steps*. In a chapter titled "Vacuum," Henry Earlforward's placid life as the proprietor of a dusty secondhand bookshop is completely disrupted when his new bride brings in a vacuum cleaner company. He watches the premises "magically whitening under a wide-mouthed brass nozzle that a workman who stood on a pair of steps was applying to it. And Henry heard a swishing sound as of the indrawing of wind. ... No grime, no dust anywhere!. ... He had been robbed of something."[17] So stingy is Earlforward that he even asks the cleaning men if they intend to sell the dirt. The gigantic vacuum cleaner that robs Earlforward of this dirt was the brainchild of British engineer Hubert Cecil Booth (1871–1955), who devised a gasoline-powered, horse-drawn wagon, nicknamed Puffing Billy after a famous steam engine, to be rented out to business and domestic premises (Fig. 2.1).[18] The present study aims to gauge the cultural reverberations of the vacuum cleaner as it morphed from Puffing Billy to today's compact robovacs.

Henry James famously proclaimed, "relations stop nowhere."[19] The relations extending from the vacuum cleaner—like the appliance itself with its nifty attachments—sneak into every nook and cranny of the modern imaginary. Indeed, the *idea* of the vacuum cleaner sucks up relations and associations as greedily as the machine sucks dust. The following chapters pursue these relations in a range of milieux: domestic, financial, aesthetic, military. Standing at the forefront of seismic changes in technology, automation, finance, marketing, hygiene, infrastructure, time-management, domestic labour, and the history of dirt,[20] the vacuum cleaner also insinuates itself into the dominant phobias of the period, including totalitarianism, nuclear war, and the "manufactured risks" arising from modern technology.[21]

While these relations stop nowhere, they congeal for the purposes of argument into a cluster of contradictions. Even the term "vacuum cleaner" is contradictory, given that no vacuum is involved in the machinery, and this misnomer raises further ambiguities: does the cleaner clean the vacuum, or does the vacuum do the cleaning, creating a vacuum in nature (which abhors a vacuum)? The verb "to vacuum"—elliptical for "vacuum clean"— highlights these ambiguities. Taken literally, to vacuum with a vacuum is to enlist non-being against being, to make nothing out of something, which implies that "something"—materiality per se—amounts to refuse.

These ominous implications haunt the cultural history of the vacuum cleaner, which has been portrayed—albeit parodically—as an apocalyptic and annihilating force. In *The Monster* (1944), a zany novel by Friedl Benedikt published under the *nom de plume* Anna Sebastian,[22] a salesman called Jonathan Crisp (modelled according to Benedikt on her philandering lover Elias Cannetti) attempts to flog a vacuum cleaner brand-named Tantalus to recalcitrant bohemian clients in London. Crisp's sales pitch intensifies from hyperbole—"our best, our unsurpassable streamline model"—to zealotry, as he comes to idolize the appliance as a genocidal dictator that swallows up everything in its path. "Oh, desert wind; oh, sandstorm," he marvels, "and a violent and bitter admiration filled him for Tantalus, who seemed to race across the carpet all by himself, devouring every little hair and crumb, filling his big body greedily."[23]

But later Crisp turns against Tantalus, resenting the machine for exploiting his hard labour as a salesman:

You have cheated me. ... For fifteen years you pretended to work for me, but you only filled your own fat belly. You got big and round and powerful while I was starving. You fed on dirt and dust while I had to carry you from street to street, while I had to lead you from carpet to carpet, wearing myself out only to make you all the more satisfied, all the more composed and shining.[24]

Here Sebastian hints at the contradiction that a machine designed to work for human beings has instrumentalized them in return, forcing them to work for it, not it for them: "You pretended to be my slave," Crisp fulminates, "but it was you who had the power!"[25] Ultimately Crisp overcomes this servitude by becoming-vacuum-cleaner: "He remembered Tantalus's face and neck. His legs became stiff and hard. ... he could feel Tantalus's heart throb in his own body."[26] Rapacious as the machine itself, Crisp turns into a "demonic Lord of the Universe and of misrule"[27] who reduces his clientele to sex slaves.

Benedikt explained to her parents in Sweden in 1944 that *The Monster* was an attempt to show how Hitlers are made;[28] in this case—the novel implies—by emulating vacuum cleaners. Preposterous though this might seem, what distinguishes Hitler's tyranny from other murderous regimes is the mechanization of slaughter, comparable to the vacuum cleaner's mechanized extermination of foreign bodies from the home. This appliance gets rid of "matter out of place"—to borrow Mary Douglas's famous definition of dirt[29]—whereas Hitler's industrialized genocide aimed to get rid of peoples out of place, peoples deemed unworthy of belonging to the nation or even to the human species. If Hitler therefore aspired to the condition of a vacuum cleaner, transforming himself into a murderous machine, Tantalus the machine turns into a bloodthirsty tyrant, monstrous but all too human. In any case, *The Monster* brings to light the contradiction between the humble purpose of the vacuum cleaner and its imaginary violence.

As Sebastian's novel indicates, the vacuum cleaner with its deafening roar has blasted its way into the collective unconscious, arousing primal fantasies of "filthy greed" and insatiable orality.[30] While its sucking action evokes breastfeeding, this machine sucks dirt, not milk, in a coprophilic inversion of the digestive process. Its clumsy mobility, together with its gassy repertoire of hisses, coughs, hiccups, burps, and wheezes has made the vacuum cleaner a laughingstock among appliances, as attested by its comic career in the movies. In the Cold War comedy *Glass Bottom Boat* (1966),[31] Rod Taylor's space-age kitchen is kitted out with a robotic vacuum cleaner that pops out of its hidey-hole to slurp up spills and darts back like a dog into its doghouse.[32] Cute and amusing, this vacuum cleaner is becoming-pet—a transformation hard to imagine in a dishwasher or a refrigerator. Who would laugh at a washing-machine except in despair at its collapse? Vacuum cleaners are the funniest of domestic appliances, as well as arguably the most annoying. Yet laughter also serves as a defence against a deeper terror of the vacuum cleaner, its uncanny animation, heavy breathing, and devouring maw. Even brand names reveal this contradiction between humour and horror, the smiling cylinders Henry and Hetty providing comic competition to the Gothic shivers of Euroflex's Monster.

A further contradiction, common to other "labour-saving" devices, is that vacuum cleaners create more work than they "save." Mid-century ads depicting housewives enjoying rest and relaxation thanks to their hardworking hoovers bely the fact that these machines were noisy, unwieldy, and prone to breakdown, typically spewing out more dust than they absorbed. Instead of removing dirt, they made it more visible and unacceptable by dragging it out of its hiding-places and spreading it around.

Hence the time spent on housework paradoxically increased because of vacuum cleaners and other mod cons marketed for their vaunted efficiency.[33]

Supposedly sparing work for housewives, the vacuum cleaner also supposedly created work for masses of unemployed men after World War I who peddled vacuum cleaners door-to-door.[34] But this supposition is contradicted by the 500% annual turnover rate for vacuum cleaner salesmen in Britain, who were usually fired within three weeks of undertaking this exploited labour.[35] Thus the vacuum cleaner saved work only to increase it, created jobs only to withdraw them, and removed dirt only to diffuse it.

Mid-century advertising emphasized the vacuum cleaner's antiseptic power to remove the germs lurking in household dust.[36] But this claim of promoting health by getting rid of pathogens is discredited by the current plague of allergies and asthma, which has been attributed to rising standards of cleanliness. Exposure to dirt, it has been argued, can acclimatize the body to a dusty, germ-filled world, preventing the immune system from going into overdrive. By extracting (or more accurately displacing) dust, the vacuum cleaner has arguably fostered new forms of toxicity, its hygienic promise contradicted by its morbid effects.

Advertisers boast about the machine's lightness—one Hoover model was even advertised to walk on air[37]—whereas users bemoan its bulk and heaviness. Like the witch's trademark broomstick, the vacuum cleaner offers the promise of flight yet binds its user to the dust beneath her feet. Even its shape is paradoxical, as artists like Claes Oldenburg have highlighted: its wand slim and sleek, like the idealized housewife coupled with it in commercials; its bag swollen and blowsy, like the disaffected housewives of reality.[38] Stiff and slack, svelte and flabby, aerodynamic and mired in the earth, the vacuum cleaner epitomizes the contradictions of modernity, in which the dream of liberation from nature and tradition—"all that is solid melts into air"[39]—is constantly dragged down by the gravity of dirt and history and embodiment.

MAKERS AND USERS

In Elizabeth Bowen's novel *The Hotel*, the heroine imagines housedwellers "living under the compulsion of their furniture," as if they had been made "for beds and dinner-tables and washstands, just to discharge the obligations all those have created."[40] The compulsion of appliances is even more inexorable. The vacuum cleaner demands a vacuumer as an electric stove demands a cook—just to discharge the obligations these machines have created. In this sense the appliance calls the housewife into being and determines her modus vivendi, her daily life governed by her own mod cons. Meanwhile the cultural implications of these technologies extend beyond their practical usage. In a recent study Rachele Dini argues that electrical appliances are "entangled in relations with people and places. ... producing effects greater than their manufacturers or owners could ever have envisaged." As a result, the meanings of such objects can "run amuck," outstripping the categories of use-value and exchange-value to enter the phantasmatic realm of the fetishism of commodities.[41]

As Dini points out, the study of material culture and its social effects has burgeoned in the past few decades, calling for a keener appreciation of objects as active forces rather than inert instruments of human will.[42] Yet domestic appliances rarely feature in this scholarship, despite (or perhaps because of) their ubiquity in Western homes. Apart from the refrigerator, which has been the subject of two recent monographs,[43] the everyday technologies of the household tend to be ignored in literary and cultural analysis. A ground-breaking exception is Dini's own monograph "*All-Electric" Narratives: Time-Saving Appliances and Domesticity in American Literature, 1945–2020* (2021), which explores the social and cultural dimension of devices ranging from toasters to stoves, refrigerators, washing-machines, and vacuum cleaners. These devices, for example, provide the white noise of Ruby, the all-black town in Toni Morrison's 1997 novel *Paradise* (1997): "in every Ruby household appliances pumped, hummed, sucked, purred, whispered and flowed."[44] These noises mark the belated advent of technological modernity to a black population formerly deprived of access to such innovations. In most literary texts, however, household technologies tend to be silenced and relegated to the background, whether by their authors or their commentators.

In *Thinking about Women* (1968), Mary Ellmann points out that religions "work like washing-machines: men invent them and women run them."[45] Religion aside, this witticism helps to explain the occlusion of appliances from the history of technology, which tends to privilege inventors (usually male) over users (usually female). An "ethos of producerism," Ruth Oldenziel explains, has obscured the role of users in the modernization of the home.[46] From the nineteenth century onwards, "inventiveness and mechanical genius became important arbiters of gender and race differentiation, at times politically employed in the argument over whether women should have the right to vote or used to justify Western domination of other cultures."[47] Such cultures, like women, supposedly lacked the mechanical genius of white men, rather than access to technological know-how. Against the privilege accorded to inventors and producers, Oldenziel insists that users are active participants in technological development who "produce frames of meanings … crucial to a technology's final application."[48] These meanings may deviate widely from inventors' or manufacturers' objectives; a striking instance is the Swedish botanist Gunnar Erdtman (1897–1973), memorably described by Kevin Edwards as "the man who vacuum cleaned the Atlantic," who hitched two Electrolux vacuum cleaners to the SS Drottningholm to capture pollen samples from the atmosphere over the Atlantic in an influential (if quixotic) contribution to the nascent science of palynology.[49] Or to take a silly example, the movie *Daft as a Brush*, a.k.a. *Super Sucker*, is a farce about door-to-door salesmanship in which the eponymous vacuum cleaner Super Sucker, which proves a hard sell as a cleaning tool, is eagerly embraced by suburban housewives as a sex toy, thanks to its ability to handle "those hard to reach places."[50]

If domestic appliances have been overlooked in cultural history, Helen Meintjes argues, this is because they are understood only in terms of their practical purpose rather than their social and symbolic significance.[51] Hence dishwashers, fridges, cookers, washing-machines, vacuum cleaners, and other household technologies are viewed by scholars as largely interchangeable conveniences, their idiosyncrasies ignored. Only when these appliances go on the blink does their recalcitrant materiality assert itself. Broken, they become *things* rather than tools, their form subversive of rather than subordinate to function. As Bill Brown observes, "[w]e begin to confront the thingness of objects when they stop working for us: when the drill breaks, when the car stalls. …" Objects, on the other hand "we look through … because there are codes through which our interpretive attention makes them meaningful. …"[52] Thus a working appliance functions as an *object* that we look through (rather than a *thing* that blocks transparency), but an object poor in meaning insofar as its significance is limited to purpose. A faulty appliance, by contrast, is reduced to the status of a thing, an obstacle, brute matter and dead weight. Every technological advance brings new forms of malfunction in its wake, and domestic appliances are notorious for breaking down. As Paul Virilio famously declares, "When you invent the ship, you also invent the shipwreck"—a principle that also applies to humbler inventions like the vacuum cleaner.[53] Built-in obsolescence, compounded by daily wear and tear, ensures that these machines relentlessly revert to thingness, requiring frequent repair and replacement by "new and improved" models.

Low-tech, commonplace, and relatively inexpensive, "white goods" like the fridge and the dishwasher lack the glamour of "brown goods," such as TVs and audio systems, which use (or kill) time rather than "saving" it. Most domestic appliances do one thing only—wash clothes, suck dust, toast bread, chill food—which limits their semiotic resonance as well as their appeal to cultural theorists and anthropologists.[54] No wonder therefore that the PC, with its passport to cyberspace, has elicited more cultural analysis than the humdrum vacuum cleaner. But as Meintjes points out, household appliances "create and communicate meaning by their presence in the home and are as much part of a meaning system in which gender and generational relations are shaped and acted out, social status is marked, ideology is represented, or strategies for living are mirrored, as any more obviously symbolic domestic object."[55] Even so, the few studies that do investigate the social and political dimension of domestic appliances tend to focus on production rather than consumption: a focus that reflects a sexist bias against housework as non-productive labour.[56]

Feminist scholars have challenged this bias by stressing the interdependence of producers and consumers in the evolution of technology. Technical artefacts belong to networks that include both makers and users, not to mention all the other agents involved in manufacturing, marketing, transporting, and repairing these inventions. According to anthropologist Bryan Pfaffenberger, "[a]ny technology should be seen as a system, not just of tools, but of related social behaviours and techniques."[57] Indeed Pfaffenberger claims that technologies are not just utilized but brought into being by their users: "no technology can be said to exist unless the people who use it can use it over and over again."[58]

Use, meanwhile, is not just a matter of plugging in an appliance and turning it off when its job is done. As Langdon Winner observes, this common misunderstanding of use as "nothing more complicated than an occasional, limited, and nonproblematic interaction" belies the fact that "technologies are not merely aids to human activity, but also powerful forces acting to reshape that activity and its meaning."[59] For this reason, Winner claims that technological and social change are inseparable:

> as technologies are being built and put to use, significant alterations in patterns of human activity and human institutions are already taking place. New

worlds are being made. There is nothing "secondary" about this phenom-
enon. It is, in fact, the most important accomplishment of any new technology. The construction of a technical system that involves human beings as
operating parts brings a reconstruction of social roles and relationships.[60]

This reconstruction extends into "[i]ndividual habits, perceptions, con-
cepts of self, ideas of space and time, social relationships, and moral and
political boundaries,"[61] all of which contribute to innovations in technology and but are also transformed under their influence. Cause and effect
cannot be disentangled: users are shaped by technologies, just as they are
shaped by "beds and tables and washstands" in Bowen's *Hotel*. But users
also repurpose these technologies, which accrue what Bill Brown calls
"misuse value" or even abuse value from these rogue deployments.[62] In
The Monster, for instance, Crisp abuses Tantalus, disembowelling his dust-
belly; and as we shall see, vacuum cleaners are also subjected to sexual
abuse in many works of film and literature. In real life, their abusers often
wind up in ER with embarrassing injuries.[63]

Returning to Winner's argument that new technologies reshape "ideas
of space and time," it is worth noting that the vacuum cleaner, like other
household appliances, was originally hyped as a "time-saving" device,
though the time-consuming labour of vacuuming contradicts this claim.[64]
Nonetheless, the conceit that time, like money, can be "saved" or squan-
dered, withdrawn or reinvested, which is constantly invoked in advertising
these commodities, has influenced modern conceptions of temporality.
Less directly, vacuum cleaners alter the experience of time through the
deferred payment schemes devised to entice consumers. Originally marketed as a luxury commodity with a high price-tag, the vacuum cleaner
remained out of reach to low- and middle-income households unless it
could be purchased on credit. In mid-century Britain the most common
form of credit was Hire Purchase or HP, ruefully nicknamed the "never-
never plan."[65] Through financial innovations like HP, the vacuum cleaner
helped to promote what Michael Tratner has identified as the "normaliza-
tion of debt" in modern finance, whereby the Victorian ethos of thrift and
saving has been superseded by a new imperative to "buy now, pay later."[66]
The credit economy replaces the traditional idea of purchase, based on
savings accumulated in the past, with a speculative form of acquisition
based on probability about the future. Through HP, the vacuum cleaner,
which supposedly compressed the time spent on housework, extended
time for purchasers, stretching their repayments into years ahead.

The credit economy depends on risk, with lenders and borrowers gambling on the prospect that the debt can be paid off in the future. This economy therefore corresponds to "risk society," as Ulrich Beck and Anthony Giddens characterize modernity, or more precisely what Beck calls the "second reflexive modernity." After the heroic age of industrialization, which brought such innovations as chemical farming, electrification, and rapid transportation, the present reflexive age now faces the risks produced by those technologies, whose long-term effects are diffuse and unpredictable. For this reason, Giddens argues, risk society, unlike any previous society, "lives in the future rather than the past."[67] This is because it lives "after nature" and "after tradition." Advances in technology are constantly altering nature, generating "a plurality of 'future scenarios.'" Such "manufactured risks" denature nature, altering the environment to the extent that their future repercussions are incalculable. Hence "the future becomes ever more absorbing, but at the same time opaque."[68]

This orientation to the future or the "never-never" also characterizes the credit economy for commodities like vacuum cleaners.[69] In the interwar years, consumers on HP contracts were forcibly "preoccupied with the future,"[70] to borrow Giddens's phrase, in that their present was haunted by the future in the form of household objects likely to wear out before the debt was paid off, or before these goods were "snatched back" by the retailers; the "snatch-back" was a notorious abuse.[71] The fourth chapter of this study shows how the vacuum cleaner comes to be associated during the Cold War with the greatest risk to the future of the planet: the prospect of nuclear annihilation.

Marketing

Where the vacuum cleaner is concerned, the conventional division of labour in which makers are male and users female is complicated by the emergence of the door-to-door salesman, an occupation that arose between the wars to market vacuum cleaners and other aspirational merchandise like encyclopaedias. Instead of waiting for consumers to visit vacuum cleaner showrooms, manufacturers hired well-spoken representatives to demonstrate this newfangled technology in prospects' homes. These representatives were almost always male, partly because of the weight of the machinery they were obliged to lug from door to door, but proverbially because of their potential sex appeal to housewives. Yet this appeal was compromised (or possibly enhanced) by the salesman's liminal position in respect to gender. Literally poised on the threshold of the feminine domain of the home, this "knight of the road" was encouraged to identify with the housewife and her struggles against dust. His masculinity was jeopardized by this identification as well as by his merchandise, the vacuum cleaner representing women's labour and, by association, women's disempowerment. Virility could be restored only by liberation from the vacuum cleaner, an appliance represented by novelist Julian Maclaren-Ross as a castrating medusa, its hapless vendors strangled in its hose and cord.

As we have seen, Raymond Carver reimagines the "primal scene" of vacuum cleaner salesmanship in "Collectors" as an all-male scenario. A more conventional heterosexual depiction of this scene may be found in Emily Arnold McCully's 1976 story "How's Your Vacuum Cleaner Working?" in which a nameless housewife, suicidally bored, answers the door to a pair of vacuum cleaner salesmen, a young trainee and his older mentor.[72] When the youth asks the titular question, "How's your vacuum cleaner working?," the housewife's reply is laden with double entendre: "The motor sounds sluggish. It doesn't purr to a stop, you know? And it drags on, so. I think it must be the fan belt; it doesn't perform at all the way it used to. And the suction has been affected. Not strong any more" (p. 26). These symptoms reflect the "energy crisis" of her marriage as much as the deterioration of her appliance (*"The Energy Crisis"* is the name of the band that the young salesman, a would-be rock singer, is planning to launch [p. 30]). This youth makes an assignation with the housewife, who contrives to shift her husband into the garage while she enjoys a one-night stand with a lover more potent than her aging vacuum cleaner. With its "sluggish" motor that no longer "perform[s] ... the way it used to," its suction "not strong any more," this appliance serves as a metaphor for either spouse, figuring the couple as a "slackening" (p. 27) appliance, while the young man represents a state-of-the-art sex machine that "digs away" (p. 42) with all the power of a Dyson Flexi Crevice Tool.

This story plays on popular mythology in which the vacuum cleaner salesman is eroticized—a trait he shares with milkmen and other door-to-door vendors. Indeed McCully's story has much in common with a cheesy seaside postcard in which a salesman for "Plug-Easy Vacuum Cleaners" greets a bosomy aproned housewife with the line, "Allow me, madam, to give you a demonstration in your passage."[73] On the darker side, McCully's story demonstrates how appliances are humanized and human beings reduced—as Marx puts it—to "appendage[s] of the machine."[74] Bill

Brown encapsulates this paradox: "the spectral completion of commodity fetishism (where things appear to have lives of their own) is human reification (where people appear to be no more than things)."[75] As the following chapters show, the personification and sexualization of the vacuum cleaner, along with the reification of its human sellers, users, and consumers, recur as leitmotifs throughout the cultural history of this appliance. On the other hand, the gleeful "abuse value" that arises from attacking or seducing this machine militates against the instrumentalization of its human appendages.

Today the door-to-door salesman has receded into a quaint memory, having been superseded by aggressive advertising, amplified in the last few decades by the internet. In British mid-century advertising, as previously mentioned, the vacuum cleaner is typically controlled by a white, svelte, smiling housewife, bonded to her appliance like a goddess to her avatar, or a witch to her broomstick. Her chic appearance implies that the vacuum cleaner is so light, hygienic, and easy to use that the middle-class housewife can do her own cleaning in her smartest clothes without getting sweaty or dirty. This image of the housewife with her hoover—or the hoover with its housewife—signals the modernization of the home, with woman and machine mirroring each other's trim, streamlined efficiency.[76]

These ads also convey the message that the vacuum cleaner obviates the need for housemaids at a time when British working-class women were abandoning domestic service for more enticing jobs. Chronologically the professional housewife and the vacuum cleaner come forth together, like Sin and Death in Milton's Hell, both resulting from the decline of domestic service in Britain. In the United States, however, black working-class women had few job options other than as "maids," a predicament reflected in contemporary advertising. In a Hoover ad from 1934,[77] two black maids in caps and aprons brag about their respective white employers. In the foreground sits a smiling Aunt Jemima figure, while across a picket fence a taller, younger, slimmer maid looks down her nose at the older woman. The caption reads, "Mah Lady Gives Me Sundays Off!"—presumably spoken by the older woman—followed by the young woman's haughty comeback, "Yeah?—Well, I Gets Part of Every Day Off—Mah Folk's Got the Hoover." While this retort implies that the Hoover saves labour-time, it also hints that the younger worker gets no full days off, her labour instead contracted into shorter hours and (no doubt) lower wages; nor is it likely that the older maid gets paid for her Sundays off. Addressed to the employer, this ad conveys the message that the vacuum cleaner saves the mistress money rather than the servant time. By mocking the maids' black patois, the ad flatters the grammatical superiority of white employers while praising their generosity in lightening their servants' loads.

Such racist ads, as Dini points out, promote domestic appliances "as a *humane* purchase for the enlightened white housewife to bestow upon her grateful black underlings."[78] Rarely if ever do such ads suggest that black women might purchase these gadgets on their own behalf. Indeed Toni Morrison, recalling her childhood job of cleaning a white woman's house in the 1940s, remarks that she had never "seen a Hoover vacuum cleaner or an iron that wasn't heated by fire"; "things that were common in Her neighborhood, absent in mine."[79] Only in the 1950s did such appliances begin to penetrate black households in the United States.

Another racist ad, printed in *Good Housekeeping* in 1936, features a grotesque caricature of a fat black maid tangled up in a vacuum cleaner cord, headed by the slogan "Is Your Vacuum Cleaner Crippled with Corditis?"[80] Leaving aside the demeaning image, the term "corditis," described by the ad as a "dangerous disease," provides an apt metaphor for the entanglement of social relations in the vacuum cleaner, which brings class, race, and gender into explosive proximity.

*   *   *

This introduction has raised themes to be expanded in the following chapters, including the marketing of vacuum cleaners and their contradictory representations in literary texts, advertising, and popular culture. Although this machine has been largely overlooked in cultural studies of technology, it belongs to an intriguing technical and social history, which is discussed in the next chapter, *Fabulous Dustpan*.[81] On the technical side, the vacuum cleaner evolved out of the mechanical carpet sweepers of the nineteenth century, gradually accruing suction, electricity, and the bells and whistles of today's cutting-edge dustbusters. On the social side, the vacuum cleaner owes its development to the decline of domestic service after World War I and the necessity for middle-class women to clean their own homes, pressured by postwar propaganda exalting the housewife as domestic goddess. The history of the vacuum cleaner is therefore bound up with two quintessentially modern professions, the housewife and the door-to-door salesman, both of which emerged at mid-century and resulted from the postwar relegation of middle-class women to the home.

Chapter 3, *Vacuum Art and Vacuum Music*, investigates the treatment of the vacuum cleaner in the visual arts, examining works by Claes Oldenburg, Jeff Koons, Andy Warhol, Richard Hamilton, Martha Rosler, Eulàlia Grau, and Kerry James Marshall. While these artists explore the visual dimension of the vacuum cleaner, composers have exploited its sonic dimension, incorporating its noise into experimental music. In Malcolm Arnold's 1956 *A Grand, Grand Overture*, for example, the conventional orchestra is augmented by three panting vacuum cleaners. This appliance also features as an obsessive leitmotif in Frank Zappa's productions. Speaking of his "oeuvre," Zappa deliberately mispronounced the word as "oovrah" or even "Hoover," this malapropism suggesting (according to Ben Watson) that the artist's whole back catalogue sucks.[82]

Chapter 4, *Nuclear Vacuum*, turns to literature, focusing on Maclaren-Ross's *Of Love and Hunger* and Graham Greene's *Our Man in Havana*, both of which promote the vacuum cleaner salesman to the leading role. *Of Love and Hunger* is based on the author's experience of selling vacuum cleaners in the bleak out-of-season seaside resort of Bognor Regis. Published two years before Arthur Miller's *Death of a Salesman* premiered on Broadway, *Of Love and Hunger* prefigures Miller's searing portrait of the commercial traveller dumped on the scrapheap: "a man," as Raymond Williams puts it, "who from selling things has passed to selling himself, and has become, in effect, a commodity which like other commodities will at a certain point be economically discarded."[83] Maclaren-Ross's portrait of the writer as a vacuum cleaner salesman shows how this appliance interpellates sellers and consumers into an exchange that crosses the boundary between public commerce and domestic intimacy.

Maclaren-Ross's brief stint as a vacuum cleaner salesman intrigued Graham Greene, who later assigned this job to the unlikely spy in *Our Man in Havana*. In this "entertainment," as Greene characterized the novel, the hard-up salesman James Wormold is inveigled into espionage by a recruiting agent from MI6 who assures him: "With your cleaners you've got the entrée everywhere."[84] The liminal condition of the vacuum cleaner salesman, hovering on the threshold—literal and metaphorical—between the worlds of masculine marketing and feminine domesticity resembles the duplicitous position of the spy, the outsider within—like the proverbial Red under the bed—who figures insistently in Cold War paranoia. Written during the Cold War, *Our Man in Havana* pivots on a comic but ominous confusion of a vacuum cleaner with a nuclear weapon. This is less incongruous than it might seem, given that both technologies were promoted as defences against the Communist threat. The up-to-date Western home, equipped with the latest "labour-saving" devices, was hyped as an enticing alternative to the backwardness attributed to the Soviet bloc, in a propaganda war reinforced by nuclear sabre-rattling.

The coda, *The House Was Clean*, reviews the ways in which the vacuum cleaner has been anthropomorphized, sexualized, and demonized in art and popular culture. As these protean transformations indicate, the vacuum cleaner's cultural meanings greatly exceed its workaday function. The contrast between its banal reality and its imaginary metamorphoses could be compared to Virginia Woolf's observation about woman in *A Room of One's Own*:

> if woman had no existence save in the fiction written by men, one would imagine her a person of the utmost importance; very various; heroic and mean; splendid and sordid; infinitely beautiful and hideous in the extreme....[85]

This comparison is not gratuitous in that phobias about women, especially in their maternal and domestic role, are often projected onto the vacuum cleaner. In Melanie Klein's terminology, the vacuum cleaner has come to represent the "bad breast," imagined as a nagging harpy, blood-sucking vampire, or man-eating monster.[86] On the other hand, children's books reassure the young that the vacuum cleaner's din is worse than its bite, or that its fury can be tamed. Vacuum cleaners can be cute—like the winsome siblings Henry and Hetty[87]—or gruff but kindly like Kirby in *The Brave Little Toaster*.[88]

The following chapters pursue these ramifying contradictions through the arts of fiction, music, film, painting, sculpture, and assemblage. In all these arts, the literal meaning of the vacuum cleaner cannot be detached from its allegorical reverberations. For this reason, I approach this appliance from both the collector's and the allegorist's point of view, showing how its factual history is shadowed by its metaphorical career as an icon of modernity.

NOTES

1. Sylvia Townsend Warner, "'Modern Witches'—Episode Two," first published in *Eve* (18 August 1926), *The Sylvia Townsend Warner Society Newsletter* 10 (2005), n.p. See also Terry Pratchett's *The Witch's Vacuum Cleaner and Other Stories* (London: Clarion Books, 2017).
2. Raymond Carver, "Collectors," in *Will You Please be Quiet, Please?* (New York: Random House, 1992), pp. 102–110; at p. 102. All page numbers in my discussion of "Collectors" refer to this edition.
3. The vacuum cleaner reappears in another strange story by Carver, "Put Yourself in My Shoes" (1972), which opens with the sentence: "The telephone rang while he was running the vacuum cleaner" (*Will You Please be Quiet, Please?*, pp. 97–110, at p. 97). Bell, summons, vacuum cleaner: these recurrent elements seem to belong to a *combinatoire* of signature tropes. According to Carver, only the first line was clear to him when he conceived of this story; he didn't know the guy with the vacuum cleaner would turn out to be a writer: Raymond Carver, "On Writing," in *Fires: Essays, Poems, Stories* (London: Collins Harvill, 1985), pp. 22–27; at p. 26; quoted in Charles E. May, "Put Yourself in the Shoes of Raymond Carver," *Journal of the Short Story in English* 46 (2006) Special Issue on Raymond Carver, pp. 31–42; at paragraph 2 https://journals.openedition.org/jsse/488. This writer is "between stories" (*Will You Please Be Quiet, Please?* p. 98) and seems to be vacuuming in reaction to the vacuum in his mind. When his wife asks what he did with his day, he replies, "Nothing. ... I vacuumed" (ibid., p. 99). If vacuuming in "Collectors" serves as metaphor for the writer's collection of the "dusty stuff" (ibid., p. 79) of life—or for Carver's editor Gordon Lish's elimination of this stuff—"Put Yourself in My Shoes" could be seen as Carver's portrait of the artist with a writer's block, the vacuum cleaner signifying the evacuation of inspiration.
4. The narrator resembles Carver himself, "cleaned out" by his second bankruptcy in seven years and shrinking from bill collectors. According to his biographer Carol Sklenicka, "Collectors" expresses Carver's fear that "he was a nameless bankrupt and drunk whose wife had little use for him, ready for the dustbin of history": *Raymond Carver: A Writer's Life* (New York: Scribner, 2009), p. 276.
5. See Walter Benjamin, *Paris, The Capital of the Nineteenth* Century, in *Selected Writings*, Vol. 3, ed. Howard Eiland and Michael W. Jennings (Cambridge, MA and London: Belknap Press of Harvard University Press, 2002), pp. 32–49; at p. 39: "To dwell means to leave traces. In the interior, these are accentuated. Coverlets and antimacassars, cases and containers are devised in abundance; in these, the traces of the most ordinary objects of use are imprinted. In just the same way, the traces of the inhabitant are imprinted in the interior. Enter the detective novel, which pursues these traces."

6. See, inter alia, Enrico Monti, "*Il miglior fabbro?* On Gordon Lish's Editing of Raymond Carver's *What We Talk About When We Talk About Love*," *Raymond Carver Review* 1 (2007) 53–72, at p. 59: "In particular, Lish chose to remove many descriptive passages providing a more detailed scenario for the stories, most traces of psychological introspection, as well as several stories within the stories."

7. It's worth noting that advertisements for vacuum cleaners appropriate religious imagery: in *Advertising the American Dream* (Berkeley and London: California University Press, 1985), pp. 272–73, Roland Marchand discusses an ad depicting the 725 Hoover vacuum cleaner surrounded by "four well-dressed women clustered in worshiping postures. ... Few representations of the Christ child ever depicted a more rapt or focused attention by the assembled worshipers. The new Hoover lacked only a nimbus to complete the divine aura. ... Modern society saw little heresy in the most fervent adulation of the works of technological progress."

8. Ben Watson, "Frank Zappa's Legacy: Just Another Hoover?" *Circuit* 14: 3 (2004) 33–44; at p. 35. https://doi.org/10.7202/902325ar.

9. Sigmund Freud, "Jokes and their Relation to the Unconscious" (1905), *The Standard Edition of the Complete Psychological Works of Sigmund Freud*, trans. James Strachey, 24 vols. (London: Hogarth Press, 1953–1974), Vol. 8, pp. 97–102. The Standard Edition is henceforth cited as SE.

10. In Evelyn Waugh's *Vile Bodies* (1930; London: Penguin, 2000), Colonel Blount mistakes his daughter's suitor for a vacuum cleaner salesman (pp. 89–91, 309).

11. Elaine Freedgood, *The Ideas in Things: Fugitive Meaning in the Victorian Novel* (Chicago: University of Chicago Press, 2006).

12. Walter Benjamin, *The Arcades Project,* ed. Rolf Tiedemann, trans. Howard Eiland and Kevin McLaughlin (Cambridge, MA: Harvard University Press, 1999), p. 211; cited in Freedgood, *The Ideas in Things,* pp. 2, 3.

13. Gábor Bezecsky, "Literal Language," *New Literary History* 22:3 (1991) 603–611; at p. 610; cited in Freedgood, *The Ideas in Things,* pp. 4–5.

14. Freedgood, *The Ideas in Things,* p. 5; Roland Barthes, "The Reality Effect" (1975), in *The Rustle of Language,* trans. Richard Howard (Berkeley: University of California Press, 1989), pp. 141–148.

15. Karl Marx, *Capital* (1867), Vol. 1, Section 4: "The fetishism of commodities and the secret thereof," https://www.marxists.org/archive/marx/works/1867-c1/ch01.htm#S4.

16. Timothy B. Spears, in *100 Years on the Road: The Traveling Salesman in American Culture* (New Haven and London: Yale University Press, 1995), p. 235n1, points out that a "sustained scholarly treatment of English or European commercial traveling does not exist."

17. Arnold Bennett, *Riceyman Steps* (1923; London: Penguin, 2016), pp. 53–54.

18. According to Jane Furnival in *Suck, Don't Blow: The Gripping Story of the Vacuum Cleaner and other Labour Saving Machines around the House* (London: Michael O'Mara Books, 1998), pp. 10–11, Booth's "petrol-powered engine sucked dust through several hundred feet of flexible tubes, which could be passed through high windows. … The most fashionable houses clamoured to have the smart red vans and attendants outside, signalling to the neighbourhood that they were giving a 'vacuum tea party'. … The job cost £13, which was equivalent to the weekly wages of a tweeny— the dirty-work servant girl. … One of the first carpets to be vacuumed was the great blue Coronation carpet beneath the throne at Westminster Abbey, ready for Edward VII's coronation."

19. Henry James, Preface to the New York Edition of *Roderick Hudson* (1907), ed. Geoffrey Moore (London: Penguin, 1986), p. 37.

20. For a synoptic history of household dirt and its social consequences, especially in the United States, see Rosie Cox, "Dishing the Dirt: Dirt in the Home," in *Dirt: The Filthy Reality of Everyday Life* (London: Profile Books, 2011), pp. 37–74.

21. Anthony Giddens and Christopher Pierson, *Conversations with Anthony Giddens: Making Sense of Modernity* (Stanford, CA: Stanford University Press, 1998), p. 208. The concept of "manufactured risk" is discussed in more detail at the end of this Introduction.

22. Anna Sebastian, *The Monster* (London: Jonathan Cape, 1944).

23. Ibid., p. 10.

24. Ibid., pp. 136–137.

25. Ibid., p. 137.

26. Ibid., pp. 52, 58.

27. Peter Conradi, *Iris Murdoch: A Life* (New York and London: Harper Collins, 2001) p. 365.

28. Ibid.

29. See Mary Douglas, *Purity and Danger* (1966; London: Routledge, 2002), pp. 44–50.

30. Sebastian, *The Monster*, p. 137. Fantasies of orality have also accrued around the washing-machine, exemplified in children's books like Richard Scaglione's *The Hungry Mean Washing Machine* (independently published in 2022) and Le'Tonda Corker's *Oh Nooooo! The Washing Machine Ate my Socks* (Kindle, 2021). If washing-machines are blamed for eating the odd sock, however, vacuum cleaners are portrayed as cannibalistic and all-consuming.

31. *Glass Bottom Boat*, dir. Frank Tashlin (MGM, 1966). For screenshots of "the Bug," see https://cyberneticzoo.com/early-service-robots/1966-the-bug-floor-cleaning-robot-from-the-glass-bottom-boat-american/.

32. A similar machine was showcased in the RCA Whirlpool Miracle Kitchen in Moscow in 1959; called the "Mechanical Maid," it scrubbed the floor and put itself away. For Richard Nixon, Karal Ann Marling explains, "the latest in kitchen consumerism stood for the basic tenets of the American way of life. Freedom. Freedom from drudgery for the housewife. And democracy, the opportunity to choose the very best model from the limitless assortment … the free market had to offer. To Nikita Khrushchev, the whole U.S. exhibition was a display of wretched excess and bourgeois trivia. … 'What is this?' asked the newspaper *Izvestia*. "A national exhibit of a great country, or a branch department store?" See Marling, *As Seen on TV: The Visual Culture of Everyday Life in the 1950s* (Cambridge, MA: Harvard University Press, 1996), p. 243.

33. Ruth Schwartz Cowan makes this point in her now-classic study *More Work for Mother: The Ironies of Household Technology From the Open Hearth to the Microwave* (New York: Basic Books, 1983), pp. 97–100. As Cowan points out, domestic modernization relieved men, rather than women, of household chores. See also Michael Bittman, James Mahmud Rice, and Judy Waczman, "Appliances and Their Impact: The ownership of domestic technology and time spent on household work," *British Journal of Sociology* 55: 3 (2004) 401–423; and Carroll Gantz, *The Vacuum Cleaner: A History* (Jefferson, NC and London: McFarland & Co., 2012), pp. 14–15. Adam Greenfield, in "Labour-Saving Technology and the Ideology of Ease," in Eszter Steierhoffer and Justin McGuirk (eds), *Home Futures: Living in Yesterday's Tomorrow* (London: Design Museum Publishing, 2018), pp. 265–73, argues that the modern home has come to be dominated by the concept of efficiency, beginning with the "labour-saving" appliances of the 1920s and culminating in the "smart home" of the "app age." Appliances were "intended to afford every class of consumer a level of service previously only available to those with the means to maintain a staff of domestic servants" (p. 268). Nonetheless, "the boomerang twist of the app age is that there are once again human beings in the loop: actual flesh-and-blood servants; merely time-shared, fractional ones. … the app itself is merely a digital scrim behind which a largely immigrant labour force hustles and sweats and bids against each other, competing for the same jobs. … it is notable how often those bodies are female, how very often darker than those requesting the service" (p. 270).

34. Cowan points out that "the central vacuum cleaner, which technical experts preferred, quickly lost ground to its noisier and more cumbersome portable competitor, in part because of the marketing techniques pioneered by door-to-door and store-demonstration salesmen employed by such firms as Hoover and Apex" (*More Work for Mother*, p. 143). Although more efficient than the portable version, the central vacuum cleaner was too expensive for the average home (ibid., p. 149).

35. Peter Scott, "Managing Door-to-Door Sales of Vacuum Cleaners in Interwar Britain," *The Business History Review*, Special Issue on Salesmanship, 82:4 (2008) 761–788; at p. 77.

36. See Arthur Asa Berger, *The Objects of our Affection: Semiotics and Consumer Culture* (New York: Palgrave Macmillan, 2020), p. 163; quoting Adrian Forty, *Objects of Desire: Design and Society from Wedgwood to IBM* (New York: Pantheon, 1986): "In selling vacuum cleaners, manufacturers were quick to emphasize their hygienic properties. The arguments for vacuum cleaners as labour-saving devices were not particularly convincing. … it was as instruments of hygiene that vacuum cleaners were principally advertised."

37. See https://collection.sciencemuseumgroup.org.uk/objects/co8412 068/hoover-constellation-vacuum-cleaner-with-attachments-vacuum-cleaner. The Hoover Constellation is discussed further in Chap. 3 with reference to Richard Hamilton's 1956 collage *Just what was it that made yesterday's homes so different, so appealing?*, which incorporates an ad for the Constellation.

38. David Hillman pointed out to me that commercials often show the vacuum cleaner's flex inching towards the housewife's ankles, evoking the image of a ball and chain, thus subverting advertisers' hype about freedom from drudgery. I'm grateful to Hillman for many other insights that I have silently incorporated. The first bagless vacuum cleaner was invented by James Dyson, who moved his company to Singapore after championing Brexit for the opportunities it would bring to British industry.

39. Karl Marx and Friedrich Engels, *Manifesto of the Communist Party*, trans. Samuel Moore (1848), p. 16: https://www.marxists.org/archive/marx/works/download/pdf/Manifesto.pdf.

40. Elizabeth Bowen, *The Hotel* (1927; Chicago: University of Chicago Press, 2012), p. 79.

41. Rachele Dini, *"All-Electric" Narratives: Time-Saving Appliances and Domesticity in American Literature, 1945–2020* (New York: Bloomsbury Academic, 2021), p. 23.

42. See *inter alia* Bill Brown, *A Sense of Things: The Object Matter of American Literature* (Chicago: University of Chicago Press, 2003) and *Other Things* (Chicago: University of Chicago Press, 2015); Jane Bennett, *Vibrant Matter* (Durham, NC: Duke University Press, 2010); Bruno Latour, *Reassembling the Social: An Introduction to Actor-Network-Theory* (Oxford: Oxford University Press, 2005).

43. See Jonathan Rees, *Refrigerator* (New York and London: Bloomsbury Academic, 2015) and Helen Peavitt, *Refrigerator: The Story of Cool in the Kitchen* (London: Reaktion, 2017). Arthur Asa Berger's *The Objects of our Affection* contains short analyses of toasters and vacuum cleaners but omits white goods, perhaps because they inspire less "affection."

44. Toni Morrison, *Paradise* (1997; London: Vintage, 1999), p. 89; quoted in Dini, "*All-Electric*" *Narratives*, pp. 243–244.
45. Mary Ellmann, *Thinking About Women* (New York: Harcourt, Brace & World, 1968), p. 93.
46. Ruth Oldenziel, "Object/ions: Technology, Culture, and Gender," in W. David Kingery (ed), *Learning from Things: Method and Theory of Material Culture Studies* (Washington, DC: Smithsonian Institution Press, 1995), pp. 55–69; at p. 58.
47. Ibid., p. 56.
48. Ibid., p. 61.
49. See Kevin Edwards, "'The Man Who Vacuum Cleaned the Atlantic': The aerosol collector and Gunnar Erdtman's attempts to measure pollen rain," *Palynology* 48:1 (2023). https://doi.org/10.1080/01916122.2023.2260437. My thanks to Kevin Edwards for sharing his work with me in advance of publication.
50. Full details can be found at this site: https://www.imdb.com/title/tt0293624/fullcredits/?ref_=tt_ql_1.
51. Helen Meintjes, "'Washing Machines Make Lazy Women': Domestic Appliances and the Negotiation of Women's Propriety in Soweto," *Journal of Material Culture* 6:3 (2001) 345–363.
52. Bill Brown, "Thing Theory," *Critical Inquiry* 28 (2001) 1–22; at p. 4.
53. Paul Virilio, *Politics of the Very Worst* (New York: Semiotext(e), 1999), p. 89.
54. Bryan Pfaffenberger, "Fetishised Objects and Humanised Nature: Towards an Anthropology of Technology," *Man* NS 23:2 (1988) 236–252, at p. 237: "in the eyes of most anthropologists, technology lies beyond the bounds of disciplinary interest."
55. Meintjes, "Washing Machines," p. 346.
56. See Oldenziel, "Object/ions," p. 60.
57. Pfaffenberger, "Fetishised Objects," p. 241.
58. Ibid.
59. Langdon Winner, *The Whale and the Reactor: A Search for Limits in an Age of High Technology* (1986; Chicago: University of Chicago Press, 2020), p. 6.
60. Ibid., p. 11.
61. Ibid., p. 9.
62. Bill Brown, *Other Things*, p. 51.
63. See https://drmarkgriffiths.wordpress.com/2014/12/22/hoover-damn-a-brief-look-at-sexual-injury-by-vacuum-cleaners/ for an extensive bibliography of genital vacuum cleaner injuries.
64. Rachele Dini uses the term "time-saving" in preference to labour-saving "because of this abiding concern with appliances' capacity to 'save' time, alter how time is spent, and conjure images of both an unknowable future and an irretrievable past …" ("*All-Electric*" *Narratives*, p. 21).

65. For hire purchase in interwar Britain, with particular reference to the impoverished working-class communities of Tyneside and the Durham coalfield, see Avram Taylor, "'Funny Money', Hidden Charges and Repossession: Working-Class Experiences of Consumption and Credit in the Inter-war Years," in John Benson and Laura Ugolini (eds), *Cultures of Selling: Perspectives on Consumption and Society since 1700* (Aldershot, Hants.: Ashgate, 2006), pp. 152–83; esp. pp. 162–68.

66. Michael Tratner, *Deficits and Desires: Economics and Sexuality in Twentieth-Century Literature* (Stanford, CA: Stanford University Press, 2001), p. 9. See also Clive Edwards, "Buy Now, Pay Later. Credit: The Mainstay of the Retail Furniture Business?" in Benson and Ugolini (eds), *Cultures of Selling*, pp. 127–52; at pp. 129–31; Martha L. Olney, *Buy Now, Pay Later: Advertising, credit, and consumer durables in the 1920s* (Chapel Hill: University of North Carolina Press, 1991), esp. p. 86.

67. Ibid., p. 94.

68. Ibid., pp. 216, 211.

69. Orwell satirizes the never-never plan in *Coming Up for Air* (1939), where George Bowling is in hock to the "Cheerful Credit Building Society" for a suburban house in the Hesperides estate in West Bletchley. Bowling fulminates: "we poor saps in the Hesperides, and in all such places, are turned into Crum's devoted slaves for ever. We're all respectable householders—that's to say Tories, yes-men and bumsuckers/ … And the fact that actually we aren't householders, that we're all in the middle of paying for our houses and eaten up with the ghastly fear that something might happen before we've made the last payment, merely increases the effect. We're all bought, and what's more we're bought with our own money": *Coming Up for Air* (1939; New York: Mariner Books, 1969), p. 15. Such are the risks incumbent on a credit economy. In *Keep the Aspidistra Flying* (1936; London: Penguin Classics, 2000), p. 74, Gordon Comstock envisages lower-middle class as constant anxiety about "Rent, rates, taxes, school bills, season tickets, boots for the children. … And the next instalment on the vacuum cleaner."

70. Anthony Giddens, "Risk and Responsibility," *The Modern Law Review* 62:1 (1999) 1–10; at p. 3.

71. As Clive Edwards shows ("Buy Now—Pay Later," pp. 162–163), in 1938 three quarters of all vacuum cleaner sales were on HP terms. Working-class people who bought on HP frequently got unfavourable terms; the Hire Purchase Act of 1938 was the first piece of legislation attempting to control abuses. This Act was proposed by Ellen Wilkinson, Labour MP for Jarrow, who pointed out that the worst abuse was the "snatch-back" whereby a commodity was repossessed and resold secondhand after the consumer had paid much of the cost. See also Ruth Adam, *A Woman's Place, 1910–1975* (New York: Norton, 1975), pp. 109–10.

72. Emily Arnold McCully, "How's Your Vacuum Cleaner Working?" *The Massachusetts Review* 17:1 (1976) 23–43. All page numbers in this paragraph refer to this source.

73. https://www.abebooks.co.uk/paper-collectibles/Vacuum-Cleaner-Salesman-Hoover-Demonstration-Comic/30218901584/bd.

74. Marx and Engels, *Manifesto of the Communist Party*, p. 18.

75. Bill Brown, "Reification, Reanimation and the American Uncanny," *Critical Inquiry* 32 (2006) 175–207; at p. 178.

76. For a detailed analysis of ads for vacuum cleaners and other floor-cleaning products see Jessamyn Neuhaus, *Housework and Housewives in Modern American Advertising: Married to the Mop* (New York; Macmillan, 2011), esp. Ch. 4, pp. 175–213.

77. See https://www.ebay.com/itm/355247430146.

78. Dini, *"All-Electric" Narratives*, p. 353.

79. Toni Morrison, "The Work You Do, the Person You Are," *New Yorker* (June 5 & 12, 2017), https://www.newyorker.com/magazine/2017/06/05/toni-morrison-the-work-you-do-the-person-you-are.

80. See Dini, *All-Electric Narratives*, p. 277. The image can be found on Dini's website: https://www.racheledini.com/post/from-electrical-servants-to-wap-appliances-race-and-the-american-home.

81. This is the title of Frank G. Hoover's history of his family's eponymous appliance, *Fabulous Dustpan: The Story of the Hoover* (Cleveland and New York: The World Publishing Company, 1955).

82. Watson, "Frank Zappa's Legacy," p. 33.

83. Raymond Williams, "The Realism of Arthur Miller," *Critical Quarterly* 1:2 (1959) 140–149; at p. 145.

84. Graham Greene, *Our Man in Havana* (1958; London: Vintage, 2019), p. 25. Wormold replies, "Do you want me to analyse the fluff?" (ibid.).

85. Virginia Woolf, *A Room of One's Own* (1929), ed. Mark Hussey (New York: Mariner Books, 2005), p. 43.

86. In a (somewhat reductive) nutshell, Klein argues that the infant experiences the mother as both a good and a bad breast: good when it's present, bad when it's absent. A splitting occurs whereby the good breast is idealized and the bad breast demonized. Only when the infant progresses from the paranoid/schizoid position to the depressive position does it recognize the breast as a whole object, both good and bad. See *inter alia*, Melanie Klein, "A contribution to the psychogenesis of manic-depressive states" (1935), *International Journal of Psychoanalysis* 16 (1945) 145–74; see also Klein, *Envy and Gratitude* (1957; London: Vintage, 1997).

87. See the manufacturers' website: https://www.myhenry.com/?gclid=EAIaIQobChMIm8_JgqKN_QIViLPtCh0aIQjQEAAYASAAEgK7RPD_BwE.

88. The independent animated musical film *The Brave Little Toaster*, directed by Jerry Rees and released in 1987, was based on a children's book of the same name by Thomas M. Disch (1980; New York: Doubleday, 1986). It portrays the adventures of five anthropomorphic household appliances, a toaster, a lamp, a blanket, a radio, and a vacuum cleaner, who set off on a quest in search of their owner.

CHAPTER 2

Fabulous Dustpan

Abstract This chapter summarizes the development of the vacuum cleaner from the mechanical sweepers of the early nineteenth century to today's electric and robotic devices. Historically, the vacuum cleaner owed its rise to the decline of domestic service after World War I, when working-class women abandoned cap and apron in favour of jobs in marketing and industry. Advertised as "mechanical maids" that could save time and labour for middle-class housewives, vacuum cleaners came with a high price-tag that necessitated aggressive marketing techniques by door-to-door salesmen, along with new forms of financing, especially Hire Purchase or HP, popularly known as buying on the never-never plan.

Keywords Hubert Cecil Booth • Puffing Billy • Carpet sweeper • Domestic service • Hire Purchase • Hoover

If the invention of the ship was also the invention of the shipwreck, as Virilio claims, the invention of the domestic interior entailed the invention of dirt. Famously defined by Mary Douglas as "matter out of place,"[1] dirt is the foreign body in the home, the unclean outsider that constantly encroaches on the inside, defiling the proper (the owned, the pure, the seemly) with the improper (unowned, corrupt, indecent). The result is a never-ending struggle to evict this intruder from the premises. In this

29

struggle, the ancient broom, which dates back at least to 2300 B.C., has proved a durable weapon, outlasting many of its mechanical competitors.

But brooms are best adapted to sweeping hard surfaces, whereas carpets collect ingrained dirt that requires more intensive cleaning. Prior to the vacuum cleaner, such cleaning entailed backbreaking labour, such as the methods prescribed by Catharine Beecher—sister of the author of *Uncle Tom's Cabin*—in the 1841 *A Treatise on Domestic Economy for the Use of Young Ladies at Home and at School*. Beecher advises that carpets "should be hung on a line, or laid on long grass, and whipped, first on one side, and then on the other, with pliant whips." If they are to be washed on the floor: "First shake them; and then, after cleaning the floor, stretch and nail them upon it. Then scrub them in cold soapsuds, having half a teacup of ox-gall to a bucket of water. ... use damp tea-leaves, or wet Indian meal, throwing it about, and rubbing it over with a broom. The latter is very good for cleansing carpets made dingy by coal dust."[2] Beecher's instructions, which continue for several pages, indicate that cleaning carpets was gruelling toil in an era when heating and cooking relied on coal—"an especially dusty fuel," as Hannah Holmes observes.[3]

To lighten this labour inventors experimented with mechanical sweepers from the early nineteenth century onwards. But these Heath Robinson contraptions were doomed to be superseded when electricity became widely available, enabling the vacuum cleaner to corner the market. Industrial designer Carroll Gantz, in his history of vacuum cleaner technology, explains that "carpets were the fundamental reason that carpet sweepers and vacuum cleaners were invented."[4] Only the wealthy, however, could afford carpets before the invention of the power loom in 1839, which inaugurated the mass production of these luxuries. Although desirable as status symbols for the aspiring bourgeois household, carpets were also "the most perfect mechanisms for collecting dust and dirt ever devised."[5] To tackle this problem, inventors attempted to devise a domestic version of street sweepers, which were equipped with cylindrical brushes, known in England as "mechanical brooms," attached to the rotating wheels of a horse-drawn cart. What these carts lacked, though, was a container to collect the muck, which had to be deposited on another part of the roadway. To adapt this technology to the home, a receptacle for gathering the dirt would need to be incorporated in the mechanism.[6]

The earliest recorded sweeping machine designed for domestic use, which was patented in England by James Hume in 1811, consisted of "a box with wheels containing a rotating brush turned manually by means of a pulley connected to a handle or crank."[7] Carpet sweepers, which combined the sweeping action of a broom with the collecting function of a dustpan, began to be marketed in the 1850s. But these machines tended to stir up more dirt than they removed—which is also true of their electrical successors.[8] Inventors began to experiment with adding airflow to the movement of brushes, but most of these contraptions relied on blowing rather than sucking, which merely redistributed the dirt, often by chasing it into inaccessible corners.

The first known instance of suction in a carpet sweeper was patented by Daniel Hess in 1860. Hess's machine used bellows to create suction and incorporated two water chambers to capture the dirt. This unwieldy invention was never mass-produced, but Ives W. McGaffey of Chicago went on to invent the first sweeper to resemble a modern upright vacuum cleaner, which was patented in 1869 and brand-named "the Whirlwind." Its suction was created by a fan operated by a crank, which had to be turned by hand while the machine was being pushed. Requiring much effort for little result, this device proved a business failure, the company reporting losses of $60,000, and almost all the original Whirlwinds were lost in the Chicago fire of 1871 and the Boston fire of 1872.[9]

The engineer Hubert Cecil Booth, who also designed and built suspension bridges, factories, and Ferris wheels, is usually credited with inventing the first powered mobile vacuum cleaner. Mounted in a horse-drawn carriage with a window to display the dirt to awestruck passers-by,[10] this is probably the same machine that robs Earlforward of his dust in Arnold Bennett's *Riceyman Steps*, discussed in the Introduction. Booth himself took credit only for coining the (misleading) term "vacuum cleaner," readily admitting that the "idea of removing dust and dirt by means of a current of air produced by suction was by no means new." Nonetheless, Booth was the first designer to combine a power-driven suction pump and dust-collecting filter in a single workable mechanism.[11] Patented in 1901 and dubbed Puffing Billy, this machine was misrepresented by its honorific insofar as Booth's signature innovation was to replace puffing with sucking (Fig. 2.1).[12]

In his origin story of the vacuum cleaner, published in 1936, Booth explains: "My attention was first directed to the mechanical removal of dust from carpets in 1901 through a demonstration of an American machine by its inventor"— probably John S. Thurman of St. Louis, Missouri, who patented the "pneumatic carpet renovator" in 1899.

Fig. 2.1   Booth's original Red Trolley (a.k.a. Puffing Billy) Science Museum Group

Thurman's machine blew air down the carpet in two opposite directions to drive the dust into a box, but in practice much of the dust was blown out sideways. When Booth suggested that suction might be more efficient than blowing, the demonstrator retorted furiously that "sucking out dust was impossible and that it had been tried over and over without success." After thinking over the matter for several days, Booth "tried to experiment by sucking with my mouth against the back of a plush seat in a restaurant in Victoria Street with the result that I was almost choked."

This breathless Eureka[13] moment inspired Booth, with the help of a friend's investment, to devise a machine to work by suction "to which I gave the name 'The Vacuum Cleaner.'"[14] As Gantz points out, this theatrical account somewhat exaggerates the novelty of Booth's invention, since both the name and the principle of suction were already in use in both commercial and domestic cleaners. Besides, the name is a misnomer: as previously mentioned, there is no vacuum in a vacuum cleaner, only "rapid air movement in a closed container to create suction," which sounds neither scientific nor catchy as a brand-name.[15]

In the event, the most successful brand-name proved to be the onomatopoeic Hoover, which still serves as noun and verb for vacuum cleaners in Britain, regardless of their make. W.H. "Boss" Hoover of North Canton, Ohio bought the idea of a portable vacuum cleaner from his relative James Murray Spangler who, down on his luck, was working as a school janitor. This job required Spangler to breathe dusty air stirred up every night by a big carpet sweeper, with the result that he developed a debilitating cough. If he hadn't needed the job so desperately, he would have jacked it in. Instead, he applied his mechanical ingenuity to devising a crude portable electric vacuum in 1907 that he succeeded in selling to Hoover's wife. Previously the Hoover family had been in the leather and saddlery business, but its prospects looked bleak at a time when motor cars were rapidly displacing horse-drawn vehicles. Impressed by Spangler's conception, Hoover began to manufacture electric vacuum cleaners the following year, greatly expanding the operation during and after World War I when he established a factory in Canada with an eye to British and European markets.[16]

Although electric vacuum cleaners like the Hoover were destined to dominate the market, their diffusion was impeded by Britain's patchy electrical infrastructure, which was largely restricted to urban areas until the mid-twentieth century. As Caroline Davidson has shown, only 18% of British households had electricity by 1926, a figure that rose to 32% in 1931, 65% in 1938, and 86% in 1949.[17] In consequence vacuum cleaners continued to be regarded as an overpriced luxury in Britain until the 1950s, where longstanding Luddism, low household incomes, fear of electrocution, and an inadequate grid made these appliances a hard sell.

Because of this consumer reluctance, Gantz explains, marketing vacuum cleaners "could no longer be left to magazine and newspaper advertisements alone, the only mass communication means of the era."

Radio transmission was just beginning and would not become influential until about 1926. Cleaners had to be sold one-by-one and door-to-door by aggressive salesmen, who demonstrated their product for women in their own homes. This followed the business plan precedent of the Fuller Brush

Company, which by this time was a successful million-dollar-a-year business using door-to-door sales techniques. Vacuum cleaner salesmen often carried specially formulated 'dirt' to place on carpets so that the full power and cleaning effectiveness of their product could be made obvious. They were personable, aggressive fellows who excelled in customer relations....[18]

Basing his study on American examples, Gantz paints a much rosier picture of vacuum cleaner salesmen than we find in Julian Maclaren-Ross, whose caustic exposé of the British vacuum cleaner business is discussed in Chap. 4.[19]

In Britain, door-to-door sales were pioneered by three main overseas-based producers, Hoover, Electrolux, and Thor, a trio of competitors that Maclaren-Ross renames Vac Mac, Sucko, and Kleenup.[20] Vacuum cleaner salesmen needed to overcome the public's qualms about investing in such appliances, largely because of their prohibitive expense, but also because of the traditional British reliance on servants. Among the aspirational lower-middle-class, a maidservant beating the carpets out-of-doors presented a more impressive status symbol than a vacuum cleaner tucked under the stairs. To appeal to petit-bourgeois snobbery, vacuum cleaner manufacturers marketed their appliances as "mechanical maids" and furnished their models with names associated with maidservants, such as the Daisy or the Betty-Anne. These names implied that the machines could take the place of human menials without annoying their mistresses with human needs: the Daisy never talks back. Even today, when the vacuum cleaner has morphed into a full-fledged robot known as the robovac—a computerized disk that whirls around the floor, supposedly dispensing with the need for human steerage—nostalgia for maidservants seems to have persisted, given that the Roomba, a popular brand of robotic vacuum cleaner, can be kitted out in a frilly French maid costume (Fig. 2.2).[21]

As previously mentioned, the rise of the vacuum cleaner coincides with the decline of housemaids at a time when working-class girls began to gravitate towards jobs in industry and retail in preference to the lonely and confining drudgery of service. Yet despite the much-bewailed "servant problem," few British households acquired vacuum cleaners or other domestic appliances until the 1950s. The minority who could afford to modernize their homes were loath to relinquish servants or to ease those servants' tasks by investing in mod cons: in fact, some employers refused to buy a vacuum cleaner on the grounds that it would make their housemaids lazy.[22] Even flush toilets were resisted as déclassé: Virginia Woolf's

Fig. 2.2   Roomba in French maid costume. (Photograph by author)

niece Angelica Bell as a child enjoyed covering "her excrement like a cat," using a tiny shovel and pan for the ashes. Presumably her well-to-do parents felt no compulsion to invest in a toilet when they could still find servants to empty their slops. As Alison Light has pointed out, the British need to be served was "as much emotional as economic."[23]

Meanwhile the British government, instead of urging investment in "white goods" and other labour-saving appliances, railed against the selfishness of young women who, booted out of the jobs that they had undertaken during World War I, which were now reserved for men, refused to don cap and apron and resume the slavish hours, poor pay, and loss of independence entailed by domestic service. The right-wing press stirred up outrage against unmarried women on the dole who "ought" to be employed as maids to alleviate the plight of middle-class women, "crushed" by household chores that were undermining their capacity to regenerate the race. The health of the nation was held to be at stake: enlisting the pseudo-science of eugenics, pundits warned that working-class mothers were liable to outbreed their exhausted betters, thereby degrading the racial stock.[24] In all these exhortations nobody suggested that husbands might contribute to the housework: domestic tasks were rigidly allotted to the female sex.[25]

Besides this lingering attachment to servants, a real income gap prevented British households from emulating the American domestic revolution. Many working-class homes could not afford carpets, let alone machines to clean them, nor were these households wired for electricity.[26] For this reason, electricity companies offered incentives for wiring to encourage consumers to buy appliances, which would increase usage of power.[27] A crucial element in utility suppliers' marketing strategies, especially where working-class households were concerned, was the use of hire-purchase schemes,[28] which enabled householders to acquire appliances while paying off the full cost in instalments over several years.

Although HP was well-established before expanding into the mass market during and after World War I, this form of credit was stigmatized because it tended to involve higher sums and longer periods of repayment than, say, buying "on tick" at the local greengrocers. HP was therefore fervently denounced by pundits like "General" William Booth of the Salvation Army, writing in 1890:

> The decent poor man or woman … is charged, in addition to the full market value of his purchase, ten or twenty times the amount of what would be a fair rate of interest, and more than this if he should at any time, through misfortune, fail in his payment, the total amount already paid will be confiscated, the machine seized, and the money lost.[29]

Working-class consumers were often so secretive about HP that large items were delivered in unmarked vans to protect their purchasers from sneering neighbours. MP Ellen Wilkinson, initiator of the 1938 Hire-Purchase legislation, was puzzled by this secrecy, especially because it was self-defeating: "Surely it was better to have a van labelled 'Furniture on Hire-Purchase Terms'; no-one should be ashamed of it, and certainly it would not cause the smiles that arise when a plain van arrives in a respectable suburb."[30] Ironically, concealment made such deliveries more conspicuous.

Largely unregulated, the HP system came to be associated with high rates of interest, inferior products that wore out before the instalments were paid off, and the notorious "snatch-back," whereby goods were repossessed after much of their purchase price had been paid off. But instead of attacking these abuses, Paul Johnson has shown, "the complaints and accusations tended to be general and ideological, like those of the Grimsby Stipendiary Magistrate who, in 1929, described hire-purchase as 'a wretched system by which traders tempt young people to get married on borrowed money.'"[31]

HP also met with resistance from conservative consumers adhering to an old-fashioned ethos of living within their means.[32] "I don't hold with hire-purchase," the elderly Miss Tuke warns the salesman Richard Francis Fanshawe in Maclaren-Ross's *Of Love and Hunger*. Trained to disarm this prejudice, Fanshawe compares the vacuum cleaner to a "mechanical maid": "After all, you wouldn't pay your maid a year's wages in advance, would you?"[33] The flaws in this analogy are swept under the carpet, as it were, by Fanshawe's sales patter, which implies that the vacuum cleaner magically dispenses with the need for housework, accomplishing in an instant the onerous tasks that a maid could accomplish only in a year—as if her duties were confined to dusting and sweeping. Despite this ploy, Fanshawe fails to clinch the deal, foiled by Miss Tuke's grumpy older sister who objects to the machine's appalling racket, as well as by the mishap of a broken belt, which occurs at the climax of the demonstration, leaving a pile of filth for Fanshawe to clean up with an old-fashioned dustpan and brush.[34]

This slapstick scene foreshadows the transition from a culture of service to one of the professional housewife who, armed with a battery of "mechanical maids," fights a solitary battle against the ever-mounting threat of dirt.[35] For the vacuum cleaner, rather than eradicating this dirt, brings it out into the open. Some models—like the Hoover in the racist ad discussed in the Introduction—contained a lightbulb to illuminate the grime.[36] Before the era of electric lighting, the kindly gloom of winter concealed the accumulation of dust, which was tackled only during the annual spring-clean: an ordeal disruptive for employers and gruelling for their servants when the household was turned upside down for several weeks to remove a year's encrustation of dirt from carpets, curtains, and upholstery. With the advent of the vacuum cleaner, this dirt—newly conspicuous under the glare of electric light—had to be assaulted on a daily basis. By bringing dirt out of the shadows, electric lighting therefore increased the labour that the vacuum cleaner was supposed to "save."

To make matters worse, early vacuum cleaners, like the brooms of yesteryear, usually raised more dust than they eliminated. Even today's state-of-the-art appliances have failed to overcome this occupational hazard. "Housecleaning," Hannah Holmes observes, "has always been an effective method for moving dust from the floor to the air, where you can inhale it. It is a perversely dusty undertaking."[37] A recent testing

programme for vacuum cleaners at the Carpet and Rug Institute in Dalton, Georgia, found that many of these machines pumped out dust in quantities exceeding federal standards for the *outdoor*, let alone the indoor air.[38]
According to Caroline Steedman, the futility of dusting is built into the verb itself, which can either mean removing dust or spreading it around:

> "Dust" is one of those curious words that in its verb form, bifurcates in meaning, performs an action of perfect circularity, and arrives to denote its very opposite. If you "dust," you can remove something, you can put something there. Viz.: you cleanse a place—usually a room in a house—*of* dust, in a meaning that seems to have been established at the same time as that of its opposite action, which is to sprinkle something with a small portion of powdery matter, as in "to make dusty" (1530), or later "to strew as dust" (1790).[39]

The double meaning of the word suggests that "dust" can never be dusted away, but only displaced and redistributed. Dust, Steedman reiterates, "is about circularity, the impossibility of things disappearing, or going away, or being gone."[40] In a recent book on dust, Michael Marder reaffirms this point: "Dusting is also undusting."[41] The verb "to dust" could therefore be described as an "antithetical" word, in Freud's terminology,[42] akin to the uncanny (*Das Unheimliche*), a word which in German encompasses the opposite meanings of homely and unhomely, familiar and strange. *Heimlich*, Freud explains, "is a word the meaning of which develops in the direction of ambivalence, until it finally coincides with its opposite, *unheimlich*."[43] But Freud's argument for the semantic circularity of the uncanny, as Steedman points out, requires considerable philological ingenuity, whereas dust "just does it for you."[44] Indeed, dust corresponds to Schelling's definition of the "uncanny," quoted by Freud, as that which "ought to have remained secret and hidden but has come to light"[45]— despite all efforts to dust or vacuum it away.

Given the circularity of dust, it's not surprising that the average time spent on housework either remained constant or increased during the first sixty years of the twentieth century, despite or even because of technological advances in the home—which entailed the additional labour of running, cleaning, storing, and repairing an arsenal of unreliable and all-too-breakable appliances.[46] Far from saving time or labour, the noisy, cumbersome vacuum cleaner enslaves its operator, condemning the housewife or her servants to a lifelong battle of attrition with the dust that never goes away. As Simone de Beauvoir famously argues, housekeeping resembles "the torture of Sisyphus": "The clean becomes soiled, the soiled is made clean, over and over, day after day. The housewife wears herself out marking time: she makes nothing, simply perpetuates the present."[47] Perhaps one reason why advertisers stress the vacuum cleaner's advanced technology is to counter the housewife's perpetual present with a chimera of futurity. In reality, the time of housework has no future and no outcome: "it serves as a whole only to sustain human life rather than to advance its progress forward; it is necessary for life but lends it no significance."[48]

Unfortunately for the long-suffering housewife, dirt has now come to be abhorred not just as an eyesore but a pathogen. Around 1880 the long-standing miasma theory that attributed infectious diseases to "bad air" emanating from rotting organic matter was superseded by the germ theory, which identified invisible microorganisms as the source of these ailments. Since germs could be hiding anywhere there was no limit to the cleaning required to eradicate these unseen pests.[49] The spectre of "Dangerous Destructive Germladen Grit," as Maclaren-Ross describes it, means that even a clean-looking house is likely to be harbouring pollutants—"no-see-'ems," as my paranoid grandmother used to call them—that threaten the health of the inhabitants. No longer merely unsightly, dirt has now become lethal, waiting in ambush for the housewife to relax her vigilance or slacken her Sisyphean labour with the vacuum cleaner.

Thus, dust never goes away but merely sneaks into new crevices or hides in air. To the extent that it does go away, a dust-free home incurs new perils. Recent research suggests that early exposure to "Dangerous Destructive Germladen Grit" can inoculate the immune system against allergies and asthma. The implication is that life in the modern industrialized nations is "not dusty enough."[50] This paradox confirms Anthony Giddens's view that modernity, having overcome many natural dangers, including diseases stemming from dirt and ordure, has generated new risks arising from the very process of modernization, in this case by raising standards of hygiene to a perilous extreme. The vacuum cleaner has introduced a sinister new risk of dustlessness, peculiar to modernity.

In this way the vacuum cleaner epitomizes the double bind endemic to "risk society," in which the conquest of *natural* perils, such as dust, generates what Giddens calls "manufactured risks" arising from the technological advance itself:

For hundreds of years people worried about what nature could do to us—earthquakes, floods, plagues, bad harvests and so on. At a certain point, somewhere over the past fifty years or so, we stopped worrying so much about what nature could do to us, and we started worrying about what we have done to nature."[51]

Now that climate change is no longer a distant threat but an immediate peril, we are worrying again about what nature can do to us, *because* of what we have done to nature.

* * *

The present chapter has traced key moments in the evolution of the vacuum cleaner from the mechanical carpet sweeper of the nineteenth century to the electric suction devices still in use today. In the mode of Benjamin's collector, I have taken the vacuum cleaner literally, summarizing the material development of its technology and its surrounding networks of housewives, sales reps, and the finance industry.[52] The next chapter addresses the allegorical dimension of the vacuum cleaner by showing how artists and composers have incorporated this appliance in their works, often for satirical purposes. Despite advertisers' efforts to glamorize the vacuum cleaner, this appliance constantly reverts from the sublime to the ridiculous. Its bathos emerges in Jeff Koons's installations as in Frank Zappa's compositions, subverting the grandiosity of "high art." A gauche intruder in the museum and the concert hall, the vacuum cleaner partakes of the dust that it devours: low, ignoble, out of place. While its familiarity breeds contempt it also provokes laughter, even in the most forbidding contexts. Wherever this appliance appears in art or music its effect is comically deflationary, even if also politically charged. The next chapter explores these effects as the vacuum cleaner is transformed from a homely appliance into a visual artefact or a musical instrument.

Notes

1. Mary Douglas, *Purity and Danger*, pp. 44–50.
2. Catharine Beecher, *A Treatise on Domestic Economy for the Use of Young Ladies at Home and at School* (1841), Ch. XXIX "On the Care of Parlors," quoted in Gantz, *The Vacuum Cleaner*, p. 16.
3. Hannah Holmes, *The Secret Life of Dust: From the cosmos to the kitchen counter, the big consequences of little things* (New York: Wiley, 2001), p. 172.

4. Gantz, *The Vacuum Cleaner*, p. 13.
5. Ibid.
6. Jane Furnival (*Suck, Don't Blow*, p. 14) provides amusing examples of early vacuum cleaners doomed to extinction, such as "the Griffith foot-operated vacuum cleaner of 1905, which required one maid to tread two wooden pedals with her feet to create the suction, while the other wielded the hose"; and the Daisy Vacuum Cleaner that "consisted of a box with a handle, wound by a boy, with a housemaid wielding the tube." As Furnival remarks, these contraptions "were more exercise machines than cleaning aids."
7. Ibid., pp. 23, 25.
8. Ibid., pp. 22–3; Holmes, *The Secret Life of Dust*, p. 167.
9. Gantz, *The Vacuum Cleaner*, p. 35.
10. See https://www.sciencemuseum.org.uk/objects-and-stories/everyday-wonders/invention-vacuum-cleaner#the-invention-of-the-vacuum-cleaner.
11. Caroline Davidson, *A Woman's Work is Never Done: A History of Housework in the British Isles 1650–1950* (London: Chatto and Windus, 1952), p. 127.
12. See Christina Hardyment, *From Mangle to Microwave: The mechanization of household work* (Cambridge, UK: Polity Press, 1988), p. 83.
13. Incidentally the Eureka vacuum cleaner was launched by Fred Wardell, a former real estate auctioneer, in Detroit in 1910. "From sales of $42,000 in 1910, Eureka's volume soared to $12 million in 1927…" (Earl Lifshey, *The Housewares Story: A History of the American Housewares Industry* [Chicago: National Housewares Manufacturers Association, 1973], pp. 287–305; at p. 301.)
14. H. Cecil Booth, "The Origin of the Vacuum Cleaner," *Transactions of the Newcomen Society* 15:1 (1934) 85–98; at pp. 85–86.
15. Gantz, *The Vacuum Cleaner*, p. 49.
16. See Lifshey, *The Housewares Story*, pp. 296–98. The cylinder vacuum cleaner was invented by a Swede named Axel Wenner-Gren and produced in Sweden as the Lux I under the name Elektrolux (Furnival, *Suck, Don't Blow*, p. 16). In the film *The President's Analyst* directed by Theodore J. Flicker (Paramount, 1967), Henry Lux, director of the Federal Bureau of Regulation (FBR), parodies J. Edgar Hoover, director of the FBI, both surnames referring to vacuum cleaner brands.
17. See Sue Bowden and Avner Offer, "The technological revolution that never was: Gender, class and the diffusion of household appliances in interwar England," in V. de Grazia and E. Furlough (eds), *The Sex of Things: Gender and Consumption in Historical Perspective* (Berkeley: University of California Press, 1996), pp. 244–74, at p. 249: Bowden and Offer explain that penetration of vacuum cleaners in the British consumer market began in 1915 and took forty years to reach 50% ownership level in 1955.

18. Gantz, *The Vacuum Cleaner*, pp. 89–90. W.H. Hoover claimed that his "great good luck consisted in finding out the right way to sell vacuum cleaners, rather than the cleaner itself. I would stock up a hardware store with cleaners, go out two months later and find none of them moved. I would get busy and demonstrate them to housewives and move the stock. Quite unwittingly, I stumbled on to the fact that specialty demonstrations were the correct way to sell vacuum cleaners." The Hoover company gradually phased out door-to-door sales, but Earl Lifshey, writing in 1973, observes that Electrolux "has never sold in any other way." Today Electrolux sells its products over the counter, like other vacuum cleaner manufacturers, but this company was still selling door to door into the 1970s. See Lifshey, *The Housewares Story*, p. 299.

19. A.B.C., "Sales Representative," *The New Statesman and Nation* N.S. 15:378 (21 May 1938) 863–865; at pp. 863–64.

20. Maclaren-Ross, manuscript of *The Postman Only Rings Once*, p. 19.

21. See e.g. https://www.etsy.com/uk/listing/1004179466/maid-roomba-and-ask-me-about-my-roomba?ga_order=most_relevant&ga_search_type=all&ga_view_type=gallery&ga_search_query=roomba+outfit&ref=sr_gallery-1-1&organic_search_click=1.

22. Lucy Lethbridge, *Servants: A Downstairs History of Britain from the Nineteenth Century to Modern Times* (New York: W. W. Norton & Company, 2013), p. 189.

23. Alison Light, *Mrs Woolf and the Servants* (New York: Bloomsbury, 2008), p. 183; see also Lethbridge, *Servants*, p. 70.

24. Ibid., pp. 179–80.

25. Ibid., p. 185. Ann Oakley, in her famous study *Housewife* (1974; Harmondsworth: Penguin, 1990), observes that household chores were shared more equitably between wife, husband, and children before the technological revolution of the home. For this reason, the mod cons supposedly designed to save labour for women paradoxically increased it. As David N. Nye has also pointed out, some chores previously performed by men or children now fell to women. "Vacuuming a rug may be easier than beating it, but men and boys had much of the responsibility for dragging a rug outdoors and cleaning it, which they did only a few times a year. The housewife was expected to vacuum at least once a week" (*Electrifying America: Social Meanings of a New Technology* [Cambridge MA and London: MIT Press, 1990], p. 272). See also Cowan, *More Work for Mother*, p. 199.

26. Peter Scott and James Walker, "Power to the People: Working-class demand for household power in 1930s Britain," *Oxford Economic Papers* 63:4 (December 2011) 598–624; at p. 603. Caroline Davidson, in *A Woman's Work is Never Done*, p. 38, notes that although 86% of British

households had electricity by 1949, only 40% owned a vacuum cleaner, 19% a cooker, and 15% a water heater, 4% a washing machine, and 2% a refrigerator. Compared to other countries, notably Germany and the US, the British market for electric domestic appliances was "in its infancy; it was only to mature in the affluent decades that followed the Second World War."

27. In "Power to the People," p. 603, Scott and Walker argue that the main motivation for assisted wiring schemes "was to increase power consumption by boosting the supply of appliances" and to overcome "'consumer inertia'—a combination of ignorance and innate conservatism regarding new technology."

28. Ibid. See also Clive Edwards, "Buy Now—Pay Later," pp. 127–52.

29. "General" William Booth, *In Darkest England and the Way Out* (1890), quoted in Paul Johnson, *Saving and Spending: The Working-class Economy in Britain 1870–1939* (Oxford: Clarendon Press, 1985), p. 156.

30. Quoted in Johnson, *Saving and Spending*, p. 161. For the stigma attached to HP see also Taylor, "'Funny Money,'" p. 164: in 1940, Mrs Tansley, the daughter of a colliery winding engineer from County Durham, objected fiercely to her parents' purchase of a vacuum cleaner on HP: "There was a man, a traveller, came round the doors and he was selling these vacuum cleaners. The canister type, and it was a good one, and it was £24. And I came home from work and me father and mother had got this vacuum cleaner to pay so much a week. Eeh, and I went crazy! I didn't speak to them for about a week because they'd bought this vacuum cleaner. It was just the thought that they had bought this on hire-purchase, and I thought it was dreadful."

31. Ibid., p. 159.

32. See Peter Scott, "The Twilight World of Interwar British Hire Purchase," *Past & Present* 177 (2002) 195–225; at p. 195 and *passim*. See also Arthur Miller, *Death of a Salesman* (1949; New York: Penguin, 1998), Act 2, p. 54, where Willy Loman, struggling with repayments on a refrigerator that no longer works, exclaims: "They time those things. They time them so when you finally paid for them, they're used up."

33. Maclaren-Ross, *Of Love and Hunger* (1947: London: Penguin, 2002), p. 7.

34. This motif recurs in the 1956 black comedy *The Green Man*, directed by Robert Day, in which a vacuum cleaner salesman improbably called William Blake (George Cole) foils an assassination plot masterminded by Harry Hawkins (Alaistair Sim). Having entered a newly-purchased suburban home to demonstrate his wares, Blake deposits a heap of dust and soot on the hearth rug, only to discover that the electricity supply is disconnected. After this embarrassing faux pas he goes on to discover what appears to be a woman's corpse hidden in the grand piano…

35. Anthony Giddens, in *The Nation-State and Violence*, Vol. 2 of *A Contemporary Critique of Historical Materialism* (Berkeley: University of California Press, 1981), p. 237, notes that the "role of 'housewife' was paradoxically created at the same time as women entered the labour-force in large numbers."

36. See above, Introduction p. 16; see also Claes Oldenburg's enlarged vacuum cleaner in Ch. 2 (Fig. 3.6), which contains a lightbulb, as do some of today's Dyson models.

37. Holmes, *The Secret Life of Dust*, p. 167.

38. Ibid. In Winifred Peck's 1942 novel *Housebound* (London: Persephone, 2007), the mistress of the house, newly deprived of servants during World War II, complains about her carpet sweeper: "the wretched thing seemed to drop out a loathsome gobbet of grey fluff more often than it picked up a crumb" (p. 58). Her former servant is equally contemptuous about the Hoover.

39. Caroline Steedman, *Dust: The Archive and Cultural History* (New Brunswick, NJ: Rutgers University Press, 2001), p. 160.

40. Ibid., p. 64.

41. Michael Marder, *Dust* (New York and London: Bloomsbury Academic, 2016), p. 12.

42. Freud, "The Antithetical Meaning of Primal Words" (1910), SE 11:153–162.

43. Freud, "The 'Uncanny'" (1919), SE 17:217–256; at p. 225.

44. Steedman, *Dust*, p. 161.

45. Freud, "The 'Uncanny,'" p. 225.

46. Sue Bowden and Avner Offer, "Household Appliances and the Use of Time: The United States and Britain Since the 1920s," *The Economic History Review*, New Series, 47:4 (1994) 725–748, at p. 733: "There is evidence that household appliances had little effect on the time spent on housework. In 1960 American women were spending about as much time on housework as they were in the 1920s." Bowden and Offer report that time-using appliances, such as radios, were much more widely diffused in Britain than the so-called time-saving appliances associated with housework. See also John Cheever, *The Wapshot Scandal* (1959; London: Vintage, 1998), in which a housewife, driven to despair by the serial breakdown of all her household appliances, takes her own life (pp. 104–108).

47. Simone de Beauvoir, *The Second Sex* (1952), trans. H.M. Parshley (New York: Vintage Books, 1989), p. 451.

48. Cited by Andrea Veltman, "The Sisyphean Torture of Housework: Simone de Beauvoir and the Inequitable Divisions of Domestic Work in Marriage," *Hypatia* 19:3 (2004) 121–143; at p. 125.

49. The Dyson website contains this warning: "'Many of us clean our homes to remove unsightly dust and dirt; but very few people think about what is in our dust, and the negative impact it can have on our health. With most household dust being microscopic in size, it is important to remove the invisible dust from the corners of our home that we often overlook, in order to keep our homes healthier.'—*Dennis Mathews, Research Scientist in Microbiology at Dyson.*" This quotation is accompanied by a photograph of a hideous micro-organism and followed by a list of "the most cleaning neglected spots," including ceilings, walls, mattresses, skirting boards, pet baskets, lamps and lampshades, shelves, curtains and blinds, stairs, and sofas. Were all these spots to be cleaned on a regular basis, vacuuming would never stop. Indeed, customers have complained that the light on a Dyson vacuum cleaner reveals too much dirt. https://www.dyson.co.uk/newsroom/overview/features/may-2021/most-neglected-spots-during-deep-cleaning.

50. Holmes, *The Secret Life of Dust*, p. 189.

51. Giddens and Pierson, *Conversations with Anthony Giddens*, pp. 208, 210.

52. What is missing from these social relations is the factory and its labour force, but my focus is on consumption rather than production, on the work of selling, promoting, and vacuuming rather than the work of constructing the appliance.

CHAPTER 3

Vacuum Art and Vacuum Music

Abstract This chapter investigates the treatment of the vacuum cleaner in the visual arts, examining works by Claes Oldenburg, Jeff Koons, Richard Hamilton, Andy Warhol, Martha Rosler, Eulàlia Grau, and Kerry James Marshall. While these artists explore the visual dimension of the vacuum cleaner, composers have exploited its sonic dimension, incorporating its noise into experimental music, as in Malcolm Arnold's 1956 *A Grand, Grand Overture*. The vacuum cleaner also features as an obsessive leitmotif in the works of Frank Zappa, who referred to his whole "oeuvre" as an "oovrah" or a "hoover."

Keywords Art • Sculpture • Music • Claes Oldenburg • Jeff Koons • Richard Hamilton • Andy Warhol • Martha Rosler • Eulàlia Grau • Kerry James Marshall • Malcolm Arnold • Frank Zappa

This chapter pursues the metamorphoses of the vacuum cleaner in the arts and popular culture, comparing its appearances in advertising, television, and children's literature to the visual arts and musical composition. In all these media the vacuum cleaner has acquired human or superhuman attributes, ranging from infantile peevishness to the megalomania of Sebastian's Tantalus. Artists associated with Pop Art, such as

M. Ellmann, *The Vacuum Cleaner*, Material Modernisms,
https://doi.org/10.1007/978-3-031-56666-0_3

Jeff Koons and Claes Oldenburg, highlight the humanoid features of the vacuum cleaner, experimenting, for example, with its prone and upright postures. Andy Warhol, on the other hand, eschews anthropomorphosis, which can become something of a cliché, in his black-and-white painting *Vacuum Cleaner, 1960* [Fig. 3.1] which pictures a damaged ad boasting "EASY TERMS" for the illustrated "FULL SIZE" "VACUUM" priced at "$11.25."

Feminist artists Martha Rosler and Eulalia Grau have challenged the sexism of Pop (short for popular, but also redolent of patriarchy) by implicating the vacuum cleaner in women's subordination. While these artists satirize male chauvinism, the African American artist Kerry James Marshall addresses racial oppression in his *Portrait of the Artist and a Vacuum* (1981), the vacuum of the title alluding to the absence of blacks, both as artists and as subjects, from Western art. The concluding section of this chapter turns from the visual to the sonic dimension of the vacuum cleaner,

Fig. 3.1   Andy Warhol, *Vacuum Cleaner*, 1960, synthetic polymer paint on canvas, 26 5/8 × 39 7/8 inches © The Andy Warhol Foundation for the Visual Arts, Inc. / Licensed by DACS/Artimage, London

showing how its stertorous noise has been incorporated in avant-garde music. In both art and music, the meanings of this machine have "run amuck," embarking on cultural adventures that flout its workaday purpose.

*   *   *

As discussed in the Introduction to this study, home appliances have been largely neglected in the history and philosophy of technology, with rare exceptions for the cooker and the refrigerator.[1] These domestic behemoths, of course, contain food, which is more appealing to most tastes than the dust and grit devoured by the vacuum cleaner. The stove and the fridge also lend themselves to maternal analogies that might appeal to psychoanalyst Melanie Klein: think of the expression "a bun in the oven"; or the "Icy Heart," the brand-name of the fridge in Harriette Arnow's 1954 novel *The Dollmaker*.[2] If the majestic oven evokes a womb, however, the lowly vacuum cleaner evokes a tomb where dust returns to dust, ashes to ashes; a deathliness captured in artist Jeff Koons's floor polishers, laid out horizontally as if for the grave. In Koons's installation pictured below (Fig. 3.2), these corpses lie supine underneath a 1950s pastel blue cylinder vacuum cleaner, which squats above them like an incubus gloating over its fallen competitors.

But the fridge and the oven are motionless fixtures, however uterine their warm or cool interiors, whereas the vacuum cleaner moves around, which gives it an anthropomorphic edge over its stationary rivals. Its multiple prostheses also make it seem more human than self-contained appliances. Like a person, a vacuum cleaner must be put together before it goes to work, its hoses and nozzles attached like suits and briefcases. That these parts are also easily dismembered and prone to loss speaks to anxieties about the *corps morcelé*, the body in pieces. Once assembled, the vacuum cleaner crashes into walls, furniture, and shins, entangling its user in its hose and wire, choking and screeching when it tries to swallow hairpins, curtains, and indigestible debris[3]—in contrast to the white noise emitted by sedate white goods like the refrigerator. Clumsy and ill-tempered, the vacuum cleaner resembles a sick baby or stir-crazy pet.

Most households in the modernized West possess a vacuum cleaner, though owners are often infuriated by its racket, clumsiness, and inefficiency. In popular culture, this fury seems to be projected onto the machine itself, which is often portrayed as a rampaging monster: as we have seen, "Monster" is the brand name of a Euroflex vacuum cleaner, and

Fig. 3.2   Jeff Koons, *New Hoover Deluxe Shampoo Polishers, New Shelton Wet/Dry 5 Gallon Displaced Quadradecker*, 1981–1987, six shampoo polishers, vacuum cleaner, acrylic, fluorescent lights, 116 × 54 × 28 inches, 294.6 × 137.2 × 71.1 cm © Jeff Koons

The Monster the title of Sebastian's novel about a vacuum cleaner's Hitlerian greed. In children's media, the vacuum cleaner has been portrayed as a curmudgeon, like Kirby the grumpy vacuum cleaner with a heart of gold in Jerry Ree's *The Brave Little Toaster*.[4] By contrast, Jeremy Strong's "Fatbag: The Demon Vacuum Cleaner" shows no mercy as he terrorizes the community, slurping up everything in his path, "[f]urious anger ... flooding his glistening globe." Fatbag and his "his great comrade," a "sinister electric lawnmower," have hatched a plot for machines to take over the world, wresting power from their human oppressors.[5] In contrast to these angry dissidents, the Henry vacuum cleaner, brightly coloured with a smiling face, paired with his pink sister Hetty, seems designed to reassure consumers that these voracious fiends are actually cute, endearing kids.[6]

Jean Baudrillard argues that the automated object's capacity to "work by itself" makes "its resemblance to the autonomous human being ... unmistakable."[7] But what really clinches this resemblance, in my view, is the vacuum cleaner's *failure* to work by itself, its abject dependence on its driver and its clownish incompetence, accompanied by all-too-human clatter and complaint. More convincingly, Baudrillard claims that the vacuum cleaner's automatism prefigures its future as a robot, in which fantasies of "absolute functionality" and "absolute anthropomorphism" coalesce. Indeed, Baudrillard claims that the robot originated in household electrical appliances like the so-called "automatic maid," which was an early advertising slogan for the vacuum cleaner (see Chap. 2).[8]

The anthropomorphic dimension of the vacuum cleaner also emerges in Jeff Koons's 1980 exhibition entitled "The New," which featured brand-new, store-bought vacuum cleaners in sterile, fluorescent-lit vitrines.[9] In addition to its "anthropomorphic qualities," Koons describes the vacuum cleaner as a "machine" that "displays both male and female sexuality. It has orifices and phallic attachments."[10] These sexual characteristics feature prominently in French commercials—true to national stereotype—in contrast to their straightlaced British and American competitors. A 1958 ad for the French company Samy features a shapely woman draped over the brand name, lifting her skirt seductively to a phallic vacuum cleaner canister. The caption "Ce que toute femme désire" [what every woman desires] appears to have been ejaculated by the machine's tip (Fig. 3.3).[11]

While this ad glamorizes the phallic properties of the machine, the hermaphroditic features noted by Koons have inspired a minor subgenre of comic erotica. The poet Bob Rosenthal, in his cult classic *Cleaning Up New York* (1976), an account of odd jobbing as a cleaning man, gets turned on by a feminized vacuum cleaner.

> I find an intimacy with the Hoover in the single-minded exercise of vacuum-ing stairs. ... I unzip my fly to see what's happening and a great erection grows out of it. Hoover is buzzing, humming next to me. ... I fuck the sucking vacuum. ... But it doesn't go anywhere. ... my best fantasy of an

Fig. 3.3 1958 advertisement for Samy aspirateur (vacuum cleaner)

obliging vacuum cleaner doesn't do anything for either of us. So I pack it in. "We came really close!" I reflect while putting the rug attachment back on the Hoover.[12]

While Rosenthal's sexual encounter "doesn't go anywhere," the hero of Rick Johnson and Natalie Alder's *The Vacuum Chronicles* loses his virginity to a feminized Hoover and goes on to indulge in "intense personal relations with every make and model of vacuum cleaners known to mankind." He confesses: "I knew how to turn on a vacuum cleaner; women, not so much."[13] But vacuum cleaners may also be masculinized, as in

Seduced by the Vacuum: A Tale of Lust and Dust by Celestia Dew (I kid you not), in which the heroine is nuzzled, sucked, and penetrated by Vic, the horny dustbuster of her childhood.[14] The genders come together in B.S. Johnson's cult classic *Christie Malry's Own Double Entry* (1973), which includes a sex scene with a Goblin vacuum cleaner, "using the full range of accessories"[15]—thus casting a startling new light on double-entry bookkeeping.

Curiously Koons's own vacuum cleaner artworks are deprived of the sexual potential he imputes to these machines. His undead Hoovers, entombed in plexiglass, are condemned to perpetual virginity. Never to breathe or pant or suck or thrust, they flaunt a sterility that parodies their function as cleaning tools. Meanwhile their collective title "The New" mocks the instant obsolescence of these commodities, doomed to be antiquated by the latest model as they persist in suspended animation, "still unravish'd," like Keats's Grecian urn.[16] In a rather heavy-handed way, Koons is showcasing what happens when an everyday commodity is transformed into a museum display:[17] for one thing, its use value is eclipsed by its exchange value, which in Koons's case has appreciated astronomically. Those 1930s British householders who balked at spending £26 on a Hoover might be dismayed to learn that Koons's readymades sell for millions.[18]

The multiplication of vacuum cleaners in Koons's installations alludes to mass production, thereby subverting the "aura" of uniqueness customarily attributed to artworks in museums.[19] Products of the assembly-line, Koons's identical machines defy the value of originality, much as their artist flaunts his own plagiarism. For Koons is by no means the first artist to exploit the aesthetic potential of the vacuum cleaner, though he may be the most meretricious. Predecessors of Koons's *The New* include the tiny collage that launched the Pop Art movement in Britain, Richard Hamilton's *Just what was it that made yesterday's homes so different, so appealing?* (1956) (Fig. 3.4).

This collage depicts a swish 1950s living-room decked out with the latest icons of postwar affluence, including a television, tape recorder, telephone, and processed food, specifically a canned ham—possibly a jokey reference to the hammy poses of the semi-naked couple occupying this des res. On the left is an advertisement for Hoover's latest vacuum cleaner, the Constellation, which was designed by Henry Dreyfuss and launched in 1954. The name Constellation and the spherical shape of the machine, ringed like the planet Saturn with a vinyl furniture guard, evoke the Cold

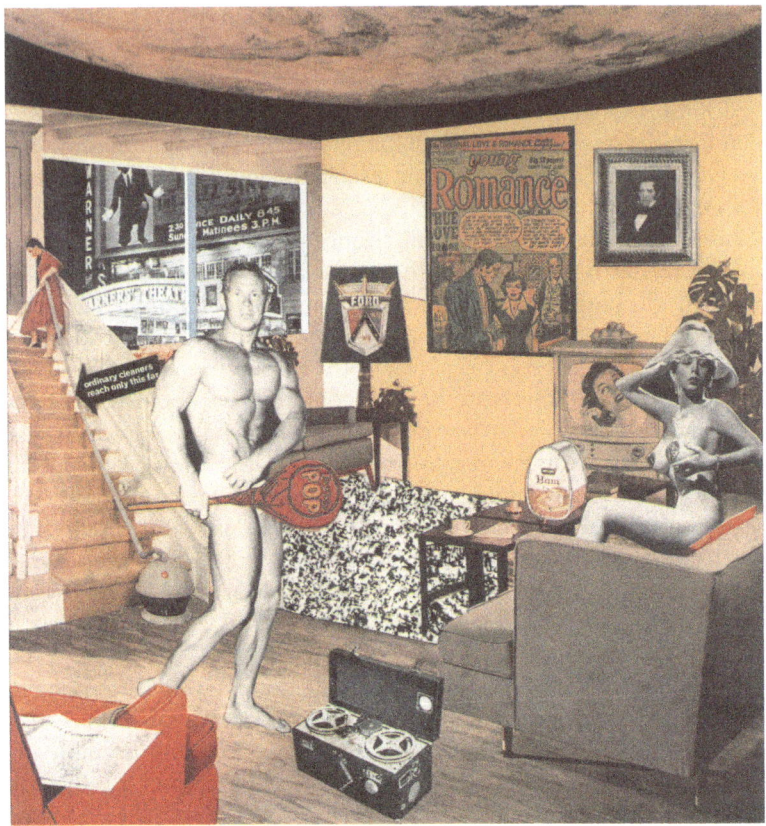

Fig. 3.4   Richard Hamilton, *Just what was it that made yesterday's homes so different, so appealing?* 1992. Color laser print 10 1 /4 × 9 7/8 in. (26 × 25.1 cm) Purchase Reba and Dave Williams Gift 2004 (2004:339) © R. Hamilton, image © Metropolitan Museum of Art. All Rights Reserved, DACS and ARS 2023

War space race, which is also referenced in the photograph of the earth's surface seen from outer space that forms the ceiling of the living-room.[20]

The most striking innovation of the Constellation was its ability to "walk on air," like an astronaut in space, floating on an air cushion of its own exhaust, which eliminated the need for casters, wheels, or runners. But instead of touting this quasi-magic power of defying gravity, the Hoover ad boasts about the length of the vacuum cleaner's hose. A woman in a fashionable red swing dress—mirroring the muscleman's red racket-cum-lollipop—stands near the top of a staircase, wielding a nozzle that disappears out of the picture-frame, while an arrow pointing down a few steps below her stylish high heels announces that "ordinary cleaners reach only this far." In contrast to ordinary cleaners—this ad implies—the Constellation's prodigious hose reaches to the stars, signalling both phallic prowess and achieved ambition, while also serving as a proxy for the bodybuilder's genitals, coyly concealed behind his suggestive "Tootsie POP." In a kind of pop culture send-up of Marcel Duchamp's "Nude Descending a Staircase" (1912), the epitome of Cubism, Hamilton's collage presents a well-dressed housewife *ascending* a staircase armed with the latest mod con. Her fully clothed figure poses an ironic contrast to the brazen nude seated on the sofa to the right who flaunts her sequined nipple-pasties and lampshade headdress. The juxtaposition of these two figures, one domestic and the other pornographic, speaks to women's dual exploitation as unpaid chars and sex toys.

In the United States Pop Art took off a few years later than in Britain, its heyday arriving in the 1960s. Arguably the leading artist of the movement was Andy Warhol, famous for his Campbell soup cans and other ironic elegies to popular culture. Like Hamilton, Warhol presents the vacuum cleaner as a hieroglyph of consumerism. Warhol's early black-and-white painting, *Vacuum Cleaner 1960* (Fig. 3.1), portrays a lopsided ad in which an outline drawing of the titular appliance, confined to the left side of the canvas, is upstaged by the surrounding bold-faced text. Beneath the vacuum cleaner's cylinder and across its hose stretches a period-setting telephone number, LU4-3083, which dates the ad to the early 1960s before those leading letters were replaced by today's all-digit format. Above this number the exhortation "CALL NOW" has been partially expunged, the first two letters whited out.

Fragmented and askew, this ad could have been torn off the corner of a newspaper, connoting the ephemeral flotsam of consumerism. Uprooted from its commercial context, its bold graphics, designed to catch the eye and whet the appetite, mock their own fanfare, making advertising look quaint and overblown. As Freud says of the dreamwork, word-presentations are reduced to thing-presentations[21] (which makes me wonder if this theory was influenced as much by modern advertising as by dreams). By transposing the ad into a painting, Warhol reduces its words to things, stripping them of their commercial purport. The capital letters "VACUUM," floating in white space, allude to the commodity but also become self-referential, denoting their own vacuous hype as well as the vacant space surrounding them.

This painting, which belongs to a series of hand-painted images reproducing bits of comic and advertising graphics, could be regarded as an attempt to individualise mass (re)productions: the dripping U marks the image as a painting rather than a mechanical reproduction. But on the other hand, the painting could also be regarded as a satire of the pretensions of individually expressive art. The satirical impulse predominates in Warhol's later "vacuum-cleaner piece," performed in 1972 at Finch College in New York City, when the artist vacuumed a patch of carpet in the college's art gallery, signed the dust bag, propped it on a pedestal, and went home. This performance suggests an analogy—comparable to Carver's "Collectors"—between the artist and the vacuum cleaner as scavengers of everyday life, collecting those "bits of ourselves" that fall away unnoticed. In Warhol's pantomime, the vacuum cleaner is both medium and message, both means and end, its dust bag exalted into art by virtue of the artist's signature (Fig. 3.5).

The sculptor Claes Oldenburg also celebrates (or ridicules) the vacuum cleaner in his visual and performance works. Famous for his gigantism—such as his 24-foot *Lipstick (Ascending) on Caterpillar Tracks* in New Haven and his 45-foot *Clothespin* in Philadelphia—Oldenburg produced an oversized vacuum cleaner in 1971, equipped with an eye-catching red bag and an interior lightbulb (Fig. 3.6).[22] In contrast to his civic monuments, however, this vacuum cleaner is enlarged rather than colossal: it seems to call for a housewife elongated to equivalent proportions, but not a giant. Yet the conspicuous absence of a human user makes the machine look heavy, lonely, and forsaken, like a fat girl in a party dress rejected as a dancing partner. Also melancholy is the machine's slavish verisimilitude: only its exaggerated scale, combined with its air of obsolescence, distinguishes it from the familiar household appliance. Given that Koons titles his vacuum cleaner gallery "The New," Oldenburg might have dubbed this abject hulk "The Old."

In a famous aphorism in *Civilization and its Discontents*, Freud observes that "man has … become a kind of prosthetic God. When he puts on all his auxiliary organs he is truly magnificent; but those organs have not grown on to him and they still give him much trouble at times."[23] If Freud stresses the discomfort of "man," burdened with dangerous supplements, Oldenburg calls attention to the plight of the prosthesis abandoned by its host. His bulky vacuum cleaner has the air of a dismembered limb,

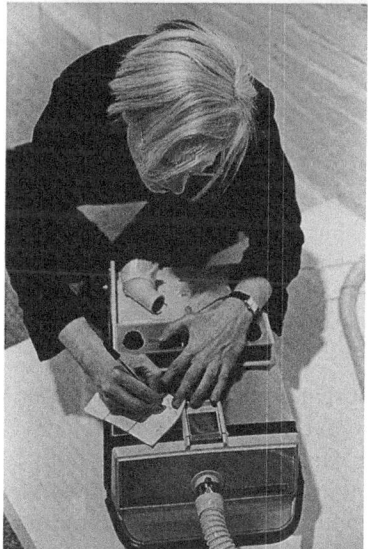

Fig. 3.5 Michael Kostiuk. Photograph of Andy Warhol vacuuming a gallery carpet at the Art in Process V exhibition, 1972. Exhibition records of the Contemporary Study Wing of the Finch College Museum of Art, 1943–1975. Archives of American Art, Smithsonian Institution

Fig. 3.6   Claes Oldenburg, *Vacuum Cleaner*, 1964–1971, aluminium, vinyl, plastic, rubber, carpet, lightbulb and cord, 64" × 29" × 29" (162.6 cm × 73.7 cm × 73.7 cm). © The Estate of Claes Oldenburg. (Photograph by Ellen Page Wilson & Gordon Riley Christmas, courtesy Pace Gallery)

amputated from an absent body. Like William Carlos Williams's red wheel-barrow, this red vacuum cleaner at once evokes and cancels out the labour and the labourer for which it was designed. Both contraptions, aestheti-cized and out of commission, stand like Freudian fetishes as monuments to lack. But the red wheelbarrow has a cheerful toy-like innocence about it, "glazed with rain water" like dew on the first morning of creation,[24] whereas the red vacuum cleaner looks worn out and comically outmoded. Incongruously colourful, its red bag seems to mock the grey desuetude of its unwieldy frame.

Fig. 3.7   Claes Oldenburg, *Proposed Colossal Monument for the Battery, New York: Vacuum Cleaner* (East River View), 1965, 12 × 17 3/4 in. (30.5 × 45.1 cm) © The Estate of Claes Oldenburg

Larger than life, though not so large as to dislodge the viewer, this vacuum cleaner shrinks in comparison to Oldenburg's two sketches for a colossal vacuum cleaner monument in New York City, one upright, the other prostrate.[25] The erect version, designed for the Battery, soars into the clouds with the skyscrapers; the second lies fallen beside the Hudson, where riverboats sail calmly along, turning away "quite leisurely from the disaster"—like the "expensive delicate ship" that turns away from the fall of Icarus in W.H. Auden's ekphrastic poem "Musée des beaux arts."[26] As Ann Reynolds has pointed out, Oldenburg's vertical and horizontal images of vacuum cleaners also reference the contrast between portrait and landscape orientation in photography (Figs. 3.7 and 3.8).[27]

Alas, neither of Oldenburg's monuments was ever built—the engineering feat is mindboggling. But the sketches defamiliarize the New York skyline while challenging conventional hierarchies of scale and value. That a banal domestic object like a vacuum cleaner, associated with women's

Fig. 3.8   Claes Oldenburg, *Proposed Colossal Monument for the Battery, New York: Vacuum Cleaner,* (View from the Upper Bay) 1965. Crayon and watercolour on paperboard 23 × 29 in. (58.4 × 73.7 cm) © The Estate of Claes Oldenburg

household drudgery, should attain the phallic splendour of a skyscraper is cheeky, to say the least; that the phallus should collapse is even cheekier. Oldenburg commented:

> What a vacuum cleaner does, wasn't important. In this case, it's more what it looks like—it's an object that could be a skyscraper.
>
> I tried to accept the fallen position as if that were the proper position—just the form of it, without an explanation of why it was fallen (or thrown), as if a skyscraper had been constructed on its side, like a fallen tree, or leaning.[28]

While Koons's Hoovers lie frozen like sleeping beauties in their plexiglass sepulchres, Oldenburg's vacuum cleaner seems to have toppled over accidentally, leaning on its swollen bag like an inverted cockroach. Has it tripped on a banana skin? Or was it felled in a terrorist attack? Slapstick or calamitous, the backstory of its fall has been expunged, and the wreck appears to rest in peace, unheeded by the passing river traffic. Instead, the slumped colossus blends into the modern cityscape, its history neutralized, like the ruins of ancient monuments in Rome or Athens. An elegy to the domestic revolution, this vacuum cleaner's undignified flop foreshadows the downfall of modern civilization, when all mod cons are doomed to bite (or suck) the dust.

While Oldenburg's designs shake up conventional ideas of scale, they also play with density, volume, and texture, typically by inverting hardness and softness. Soft pastries harden into plaster; hard typewriters soften into billowing sacks. Limp and deflated, Oldenburg's soft machines represent a eulogy to detumescence, inverting the conventional overvaluation of firmness and verticality. Both funny and unnerving, these sculptures sag like aging bodies, osteoporotic, sarcopenic, impotent. They are sad sacks: as Barbara Rose points out in a 1967 review of Oldenburg's work, "There is a certain poignancy in the melancholy exhaustion of the droopy telephones...."[29] Poignancy, yes, but also rueful humour as we recognize ourselves in these lumpy blobs. Because they are "like us," Rose observes, they are "unthreatening, friendly even," and "we cannot consider them alien."[30] Grotesque reminders of our slackening flesh, they are also cuddly and vulnerable, like huggable grannies. Gleefully embracing the pathetic fallacy, Oldenburg "sees objects as tired and as scarred as people."[31] He also sees them as gendered and erotic, his soft sculptures a flabby mass of love-handles. In direct opposition to Cubist sculpture, which transforms the human body into a metallic machine in a paranoid reaction to industrialism and alienation, Oldenburg humanizes the machine, portraying it as flaccid, out of shape, and reassuringly familiar.

To my knowledge, Oldenburg never designed a soft vacuum cleaner, perhaps because this appliance is already soft and hard at once, its rigid power head and steering rod hitched up to its squashy bag, floppy hose, and wiggly flex. Indeed, a vacuum cleaner carries its sad sack with it, however perky its telescopic wand. Given that "the best objects," according to Oldenburg, are both male and female, the hermaphroditic vacuum cleaner suits his purpose, combining as it does a phallic shaft with a womb-like dust bag.[32]

VACUUMING POP ART

Evidently Oldenburg values the vacuum cleaner not for what it does but for what it looks like: a principle that he extends to the other mass-produced machines and gizmos, usually antique or obsolescent, elegized in his artworks. A propos of these objects, Oldenburg comments: "As time goes by and things they represent vanish from daily use, their purely formal characteristics will be more evident: Time will undress them."[33] Oldenburg's sculpture speeds up this process of undressing, creating what one commentator calls a "cemetery of the mechanical world." "It is the forms that count," Oldenburg insists, rather than their functions.[34]

This emphasis of form over function, however, hints that Oldenburg was less than assiduous about housework, preferring to fetishize the vacuum cleaner than to clean the floors with it. Indeed, his soft sculptures depended on a gendered division of labour in which his then wife Patty Mucha undertook the task of sewing the sailcloth. As Rose explains:

First [Oldenburg] makes a model of the object he wishes to reproduce, then he makes a pattern with stencils, which is transferred to the material to be used; the stencilled shapes are cut out and sewn together (usually by Oldenburg's wife) and finally stuffed by Oldenburg, who fixes the actual form of the work by modeling it from within ... the opposite of conventional modeling through building up clay or wax ... or cutting away from a solid block.[35]

No stuffing without sewing: this novel technique depends on the unsung seamstress who doesn't even earn a name in Rose's parenthesis. "It was really clear from the start that there was only room for one artist and he considered himself the artist," explains Mucha, who expended her own artistic talent on stitching up her husband's *Hamburger* and *Soft Switches*.[36]

"There was no space for women in Pop," artist Martha Rosler recalls.[37] Tellingly the only works of Pop Art to portray a working vacuum cleaner, rather than a towering monolith or a decommissioned corpse, were created by women artists Rosler and Eulàlia Grau. Rosler's photomontage *Woman with Vacuum or Vacuuming Pop Art* (from the series *Body Beautiful, or Beauty Knows No Pain*, c. 1966–72: Fig. 3.9) features a smartly dressed maid or housewife vacuuming a Pop Art gallery with a machine resembling a Hoover Constellation.[38] This machine's hose encircles the woman's body like a noose, accentuating the confinement of the

Fig. 3.9   Martha Rosler, *Woman with Vacuum, or Vacuuming Pop Art*, from the series *Body Beautiful, or Beauty Knows No Pain*, c. 1966–72, photomontage © Martha Rosler. (Courtesy of the artist and Mitchell-Innes & Nash, New York)

narrow corridor, flanked by Pop Art canvases, in which her slender figure is immured. Rosler's photomontage insinuates that Pop Art depends on women's labour—somebody's gotta do the vacuuming—as well as on their sexual allure: a massive canvas of a pouting blonde in sunglasses, the creation of Pop artist Tom Wesselmann, looms on the righthand wall over the improbably trim and smiling menial. The title of the Rosler's work carries a further irony: by "vacuuming Pop art," the woman is vacuuming what is already vacuous. Pop Art vacuums popular culture to showcase its vacuity. The parted lips of Wesselmann's dumb blonde, forming a black hole in the middle of the portrait, seem to open a vacuum in which depth and history are sucked away.

The vacuum cleaner reappears in Rosler's photomontage *Cleaning the Drapes* from the series *House Beautiful: Bringing the War Home* (1967–72) (Fig. 3.10).[39] In this image, a svelte young woman with a trendy 1960s pixie haircut is applying the nozzle of a vacuum cleaner to heavy chintz curtains. Half drawn aside, their billowing folds frame a black-and-white image—apparently invisible to the cheery housewife—showing two helmeted soldiers surrounded by a rocky barricade, their pointed rifles mirroring the vacuum cleaner's spiky wand. Rosler's *House Beautiful* series was launched as a protest against the Vietnam War, but this blurry interpolated battle scene, unidentified in time or place, could refer to any and all wars, and particularly to World War I: an allusion clinched by the

Fig. 3.10   Martha Rosler, *Cleaning the Drapes*, from the series *House Beautiful: Bringing the War Home*, c. 1967–72, photomontage © Martha Rosler. (Courtesy of the artist and Mitchell-Innes & Nash, New York)

soldier smoking a cigarette—an iconic image of trench warfare—while the other soldier anxiously surveys the combat zone. Writing about *Bringing the War Home* in her 1994 essay "Place, Position, Power, Politics," Rosler recalls her motives for turning from sculpture to photomontage:

> what I wanted wasn't *physical* presence but an imaginary space in which different tales collided ... It was the symbolic collision that had attracted me. ... I began making agitational works 'about' the Vietnam War, collaging magazine images of the casualties and combatants of the war—usually by noted war photographers in mass market magazines—with magazine images that defined an idealized middle-class life at home. I was trying to show that the 'here' and the 'there' of our world picture, defined by our naturalized accounts as separate or even opposite, were one.

Some of these works, she adds, "contrasted women's domestic labor with the 'work' of soldiers":[40] a contrast epitomized in *Cleaning the Drapes*. In this image as in other compositions in the series, the Vietnam War comes home to American suburbia, invading its affluent kitchens, living rooms, and bedrooms with photographic insets of combatants and carnage. Instead of "drawing a veil" over this violence, or vacuuming it out of the picture, Rosler's housewife pulls aside the ideological curtain that contains and conceals the proxy wars of American imperialism.

Like Rosler in *Vacuuming Pop Art*, the Catalan artist Eulàlia Grau takes a feminist swipe at the vacuum cleaner in *Aspiradora* (1973), part of a series of works in photographic emulsion and paint titled *Etnografia*.[41] In *Aspiradora* a shiny mannequin, dressed in a bridal gown with pink trimmings, lies stiffly on a carpet under the wide nozzle of an AEG Vario vacuum cleaner, which looms menacingly over her supine figure. The all too obvious message is that the bride is being sucked up into the instrument of her own enslavement as an unpaid skivvy, conned by the compounded ideologies of Francoism, capitalism, and Catholicism. After the Spanish Republic fell in 1939, the Franco regime forced women back into the home, barring them from most professions and restricting them to the traditional Catholic role of motherhood. Even more sexist than Nazi Germany, Francoist Spain turned women into wards and captives, forbidden to work outside the home without the permission of their menfolk, while husbands enjoyed the legal right to murder unfaithful wives. Although these draconian laws had eased by the 1970s when *Aspiradora*

Fig. 3.11   Eulàlia
Grau, *Aspiradora
(Etnografia)*, 1973,
photographic emulsion,
anilines and acrylic on
canvas, 164 × 110 cm ©
Eulàlia Grau, VEGAP,
Barcelona

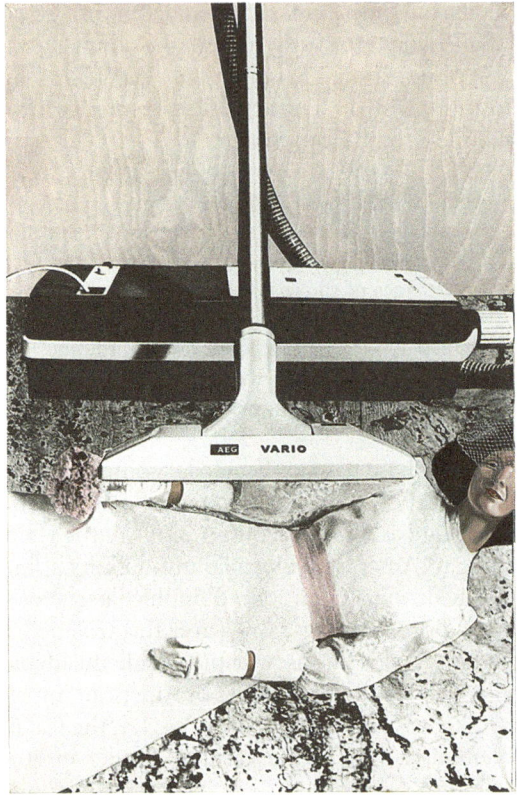

was produced, the threat encoded in Grau's photomontage looks less
hyperbolic in the context of the Francoist dictatorship (Fig. 3.11).

While Rosler and Grau have used the vacuum cleaner to expose the
predicament of women in consumer capitalism, the African American artist Kerry James Marshall addresses racial injustice in his "Portrait of the
Artist and a Vacuum" (1981) (Fig. 3.12). This painting depicts an empty,
windowless red room where a yellow vacuum cleaner tilts like a leaning
tower, unplugged and unpiloted. Inset within this framed enclosure hangs
a framed copy of Kerry's earlier *Portrait of the Artist as a Shadow of his
Former Self* (1980), a caricature in blackface with a gap-toothed grin, reminiscent of *Mad* magazine's Alfred E. Neuman. Black on a black

Fig. 3.12 Kerry James Marshall, *Portrait of the Artist & a Vacuum*, 1981. Acrylic on paper, 62 1/2 × 52 3/8 × 2 inches (158.8 × 133 × 5.1 cm). Collection of the Nasher Museum of Art at Duke University, Durham, North Carolina. Museum purchase with additional funds provided by Nailya Alexander; Maya and Anatol Bekkerman; Jeff Bliumis; Henry and Ludmila Elinson; Dr. Robert E. Falcone; Mr. and Mrs. Robert L. Fromer; Alexandre Gertsman; Marilyn J. Holmes; INTART—International Foundation of Russian & Eastern-European Art, Inc.; Vladimir Kanevsky; Virginia Kinzey; Jacques Leviant; Innessa Levkova-Lamm; Dr. Boris Lipovsky; Mina E. Litinsky; Fran and Robert Malina; Teresa and Joseph Masarich; Marjorie Pfeffer; Anthony T. Podesta; Maya and Michael Polsky; Estate of Alek Rapoport; Vladimir Rapoport; Mrs. W. A. Y. Sargent in memory of Dr. Winston Sargent; Natalia Sokov; Amelie McAlister Upshur in 1938 in honor of Duke University's Centennial Celebration; Gibby and Buz Waitzkin; and Drs. Irene and Alex Valger, by exchange; 2011.23.1. © Kerry James Marshall. (Image courtesy of the Nasher Museum of Art at Duke University)

background, this face recedes into the surrounding darkness, almost invisible apart from the startling whiteness of its eyeballs, shirt-collar, and jack-o-lantern teeth.

Marshall has explained that this image was inspired by Ralph Ellison's *Invisible Man* (1952), whose narrator famously declares: "I am an invisible man. No, I am not a spook like those who haunted Edgar Allan Poe; nor am I one of your Hollywood-movie ectoplasms. ... I am invisible, understand, simply because people refuse to see me."[42] Bearing little resemblance to the artist except as a racist parody, Marshall's "Portrait of the Artist as a Shadow of his Former Self" signals the obliteration of black experience. The human figure disappears into the shadows of the painting just as black lives disappear into the shadows of unrecorded history: "Blackness in its might at last. Where no more to be seen," in Samuel Beckett's words.[43] Comparable to the dark paintings in the Rothko Chapel in Houston, Texas,[44] which resist the viewer's gaze, Marshall's portrait withdraws from sight, blinding the viewer to everything except the white portions of the canvas. Those portions are reflected in the white prongs of the vacuum cleaner's disconnected plug—as if the figure's missing teeth had been repurposed for connecting this appliance. Note that George Washington, the much-lauded "father of the nation," purchased teeth from enslaved "Negroes" at Mount Vernon, probably for use in his own dentures.[45]

The vacuum of the title may refer to many absences, most obviously the depopulated room or museum gallery surrounding the abandoned vacuum cleaner, as well as the evacuation of the black artist from the pantheon of Western art. By echoing Joyce's *A Portrait of the Artist as a Young Man*, Kerry's title encourages us to hear "as" in place of "and"— Portrait of the Artist *as* a Vacuum—thereby aligning the artist with the vacuum cleaner but also with the *vacuum* in which black art has been sucked away. Both the eponymous appliance and the framed "portrait of the artist" are emphatically unreal—flattened and cartoonish—the yellow vacuum cleaner as unlikely as a yellow submarine and possibly alluding to the Beatles' 1966 hit. Although tending to abstraction, this work retains an allegiance to figurative painting, Marshall explaining that the black figure has already been erased from Western art: "I understood on some level that the abandonment of the black figure was a kind of loss...." What he paints instead is the erasure itself, capturing the figure's disappearance into the darkness behind its Cheshire-cat grin. The painting's enigmatic title could imply that the black artist has been vacuumed out of the art world, or that the artist *as* a vacuum [cleaner] is condemned to vacuuming that world—like Rosler's cheery skivvy in the Pop gallery—rather than producing masterpieces.

In Kerry's later portrait in this series, "Silence is Golden" (1986), a matt black grinning face hollows out a vacuum in the deep green brushstrokes of the background.[46] The brightly coloured patchwork panel on the right side of the painting, containing several allusions to Marshall's previous works as well as to symbols of black empowerment, has the effect of deepening the darkness of the portrait. Two fingers with tooth-like nails press against invisible lips, bidding the viewer to shush. Black on black, these fingers create a gap where the tongue should be, so that the face may be understood as both silenced and silencing. Suggesting a lingual amputation, the black hole in the skeletal grin marks the muting of black lives, as well as the muteness of the art of painting.[47]

Vacuum Music

If only the vacuum cleaner were as mute as its visual representations. The artworks discussed above showcase the vacuum cleaner's looks but inevitably cancel out its ear-splitting noise, which cannot be conveyed directly in visual form. Those obliged to work with vacuum cleaners, however, rather than to gaze at them aesthetically, tend to find this din their most annoying feature. Cats scurry off in terror at the approach of this huffing, puffing monster as it clatters across the floor, banging into chair and table legs and knocking over wobbly tchotchkes. Given its signature cacophony, a silent vacuum cleaner, such as those depicted in the media of painting, sculpture, and photography, has something of the same uncanniness as Edvard Munch's "The Scream" (1893), where the sound of screaming is conveyed by the mute image of open mouth and the silent ripples that agitate the landscape. Deprived of its stertorous breath, a vacuum cleaner is struck dumb, a muffled shadow of its deafening voracity.

Among the visual artists associated with Pop, only Oldenburg made use of the vacuum cleaner's roar, which provided the soundtrack for some of his famous "happenings." But Oldenburg neglected its sonic potential as a breathing machine. In his enlarged vacuum cleaner of 1971, the red bag remains permanently deflated, emptied of its power of respiration. This power re-emerges, however, in Oldenburg's *Icebag Scale B Yellow* of 1971, which is designed to inhale and exhale.[48] "An oversized, mechanical version of the classic headache remedy," as Karen Rosenberg describes it, the

Icebag "inflates and deflates with a hypnotic twisting motion and a mechanical sigh, soothing the art world's collective hangover."[49] Sighing, however, is the only sound emitted by the Icebag, whereas the vacuum cleaner's pneumatic repertoire extends to wheezing, snoring, whooshing, whining, sneezing, snuffling, belching, screeching, whistling, puffing, coughing, snorting, gasping, choking, slurping, hissing, rasping, buzzing, booming, blasting, panting, hiccupping, and farting. Regarding the last, Leopold Bloom's notorious fart in James Joyce's *Ulysses*, onomatopoeically rendered as "Pprrpffrrppffff," could also transliterate the percussive breathing of a vacuum cleaner, especially when it gags on what it sucks.[50]

As its breathy repertoire reveals, the vacuum cleaner is a wind instrument, though its musical potential has rarely been tapped. A notable exception is *A Grand, Grand Overture* by Malcolm Arnold, an orchestral arrangement that premiered on 13 November 1956 at London's Festival Hall. At the climax of this work, three noisy vacuum cleaners and a floor polisher drown out the conventional instruments. This mechanical fanfare is followed by a peal of rifle shots, which topple the appliance-players one by one, silencing each of their machines in turn so that the "real" music can continue.[51]

This musical joke harks back to Luigi Russolo, the futurist painter and author of the 1913 manifesto "The Art of Noise" (*"L'arte dei rumori"*), which celebrates the industrial revolution for introducing new noises into the modern soundscape. The "rumblings and rattlings of engines," "the stridency of mechanical saws," "the different roars of railroad stations, iron foundries, textile mills, printing houses, power plants and subways," along with "the very new noises of modern warfare": this concert of machinery moves us more deeply, Russolo mischievously asserts, than the symphonies of Beethoven or Wagner.[52] Notably Russolo's list focuses on the public rather than the private sphere, excluding the voices of home appliances, such as the vacuum cleaner's roar or the refrigerator's hum, which in 1913 were yet to become ubiquitous. Typical of Futurism's macho values, industry and warfare, rather than domestic acoustics, provide the heroic music of modernity. Russolo strove to emulate this music by inventing twenty-seven Intonarumori (noise-machines) named after the sounds that they produced: *"howling, thunder, crackling, crumpling, exploding, gurgling, buzzing and hissing."*[53]

Russolo's French contemporary Edgard Varèse also challenged the cordon sanitaire dividing noise from music. "To stubbornly conditioned ears," Varèse argued, "anything new in music has always been called noise," for noise "is any sound one doesn't like." Determined to "fight for the liberation of sound and for my right to make music with any sound and all sounds," Varèse introduced sirens and other mechanical racket into his compositions.[54] The breathy music of the vacuum cleaner, however, never features in Varèse's repertoire, and it was left to his disciple Frank Zappa to make up for this omission. In "Edgard Varèse: The Idol of My Youth," Zappa recalls his teenage fascination with the avant-garde composer who "looked like a mad scientist." Searching for information on his idol, Zappa was informed by the local librarian that Varèse "probably wasn't a Major Composer." Contemptuous of this epithet, Zappa claims, "For real achievement, nothing beats TOTAL OBSCURITY."[55]

As mentioned in the Introduction, Zappa's oeuvre could be seen as a long sonata to the hoover, which Zappa pronounced as a homonym of oeuvre. "Sold from door to door," Ben Watson comments, "the Hoover is the iconic 1950s consumer-society commodity."[56] Zappa himself undertook a stint as a door-to-door salesman, though he peddled encyclopaedias rather than hoovers. But his later collaborator Captain Beefheart, formerly known as Don Van Vliet, was by his own account "the best vacuum cleaner salesman in southern California."

> I used to work door to door. One day I knocked on a door and a tall gaunt man appeared. He had an English accent and he looked like a bird. I recognised him at once. I'd read Brave New World. It was Aldous Huxley. I couldn't do my usual sales patter so I pointed at the vacuum cleaner at my feet and said, "Sir! This sucks!"[57]

The gatefold of Zappa's 1969 album *Hot Rats* features Captain Beefheart holding up a rocket-shaped vacuum cleaner "like a priest distributing the communion wafer."[58] Other images on this cover show Beefheart coiling a vacuum cleaner's flex into a hat, and Bill Harkleroad (Zoot Horn Rollo) riding a vacuum cleaner like a witch on a broomstick phallicized to gargantuan proportions:[59] a probable allusion to the closing sequence of Stanley Kubrick's *Dr. Strangelove* (1964), where Slim Pickens as Major Kong rides a torpedo like a bucking bronco into nuclear annihilation.

Hot Rats was followed in 1970 by Zappa's solo album *Chunga's Revenge*, the gatefold of which was designed by Cal Schenkel to illustrate Zappa's unreleased liner notes: "A Gypsy mutant industrial vacuum cleaner dances about a mysterious night time camp fire. Festoons. Dozens of imported castanets, clutched by the horrible suction of its heavy duty hose, waving with marginal erotic abandon in the midnight autumn air."[60] Of the title track "Chunga's Revenge," Zappa's notes explain: "This is the music to picture the vacuum cleaner dancing to. Think of where it sweats when it gets excited."[61] In Zappa's zany film *200 Motels*, released the following year in 1971, the Mothers' road manager Dick Barber dons the uncomfortable costume of the gypsy mutant vacuum cleaner with which Motorhead falls madly in love.

Vacuum cleaners reappear in Zappa's rock opera *Joe's Garage* (1979), in which the title character seeks redemption "from the swirling cesspool of his own steaming desires" by donating fifty bucks to the First Church of Appliantology, owned by L. Ron Hoover: a spoof on the cult of Scientology and its guru L. Ron Hubbard. Hoover diagnoses Joe as "a latent appliance fetishist"[62] and advises him to go into "The Closet," a club filled with oversexed appliances. Here Joe falls in love with Sy Borg, a "Model XQJ-37 Nuclear Powered Pansexual Roto-Plooker," who looks like "a cross between an industrial vacuum cleaner and a chrome piggy bank with marital aids stuck all over its body."[63] Their affair comes to an abrupt end when Joe's "golden shower" causes Sy Borg to short-circuit. According to Nigey Lennon, author of the memoir *Being Frank: My Time with Frank Zappa*, Zappa himself indulged in Joe's appliance fetishism, cavorting in private much as he does in a notorious 1971 documentary where he applies a vacuum cleaner to Lucy Offerall's breasts and genitals.[64] Lennon remembers:

> there was an element of madness in his refusal to accept any boundaries whatsoever, sexually or otherwise. He could find erotic possibilities in the least likely situations—the more absurd, the better; the further he could push the envelope, the more he liked it. And all the while he was pushing it, he was laughing ... not too loud, but very deeply.[65]

Evidently polymorphously perverse, Zappa nonetheless shows a curious fidelity to the vacuum cleaner as his eroticized appliance of choice. Nor does he neglect the vacuum cleaner's primary attachment, the door-to-door salesman, who makes a cameo appearance in the 1984 album *The Perfect Stranger*, the title track of which was commissioned and conducted by Pierre Boulez. As Ben Watson explains, "The Perfect Stranger".

portrays a vacuum-cleaner salesman attempting to interest a slovenly house-wife in his wares. Zappa's story ("the housewife's eyebrows going up and down as she spies the nozzle through the ruffled curtain") transforms high-art abstraction into cartoon music. As a representative of the "spiritual qualities of chrome, rubber, electricity and household tidiness", the sales-man sprinkles "demonstration dirt" on the rug before hoovering it up again.[66]

The vacuum cleaner—hypostasis of "chrome, rubber, electricity and household tidiness"—epitomizes Zappa's love-hate relationship with American suburbia, its shiny, antiseptic, rubberized, high-tech banality. According to Watson, the obsessive recurrence of the vacuum cleaner in Zappa's work signals an "attempt to hoover up every music under the sun," while "sucking in all the flotsam and detritus of mass-produced 'civi-lization.'" Watson also proposes that Zappa's musical iconoclasm creates a kind of vacuum or black hole: "an empty space for the chance encounter of fragments of the external world, an objective frame in which we can make our own observations and discoveries."[67] But this optimistic inter-pretation underplays the satirical force of the vacuum cleaner in Zappa's work and its mockery of human exceptionalism, particularly in the realm of sex. Just as Zappa reduces his oeuvre to a hoover, so his gypsy mutant vacuum cleaner reduces the human body to a blowing and sucking machine.

This chapter has shown how artists have used and abused the vacuum cleaner to produce an ambivalent critique of commodity fetishism. Ambivalent because these representations, by placing the appliance in the spotlight, reinforce its cultural predominance even as they mock its trivial-ity. Koons's installations could be interpreted as either eulogies or parodies of the vacuum cleaner and everything it represents in the commercial sphere: commodification, Taylorization, sterilization, mechanization, rei-fication. Is Koons putting these machines to death or embalming them to be revered like Lenin's corpse? Even the iconoclasm of Rosler and Grau carries a sting in its tail (or hose) insofar as their works reaffirm the power of the icon by attacking it. Their blasphemy is an inverted form of rever-ence. As for Zappa, his love affair with the vacuum cleaner, evident in both his oeuvre and his sex life, defuses any intended censure of commodity capitalism. If Joe of *Joe's Garage* is a convert to Appliantology, his creator is an unabashed appliantophile.

*   *   *

The next chapter turns from music and the visual arts to literature, examining two novels concerned with vacuum cleaners and their salesmen, Maclaren-Ross's *Of Love and Hunger* and Graham Greene's *Our Man in Havana*. Regarding Benjamin's distinction between the collector and the allegorist, *Of Love and Hunger* lends itself to both approaches. To the collector, the novel offers a documentary exposé of selling vacuum cleaners door-to-door, that inglorious profession that Maclaren-Ross took up briefly in financial desperation. So true to fact is Maclaren-Ross's account of the conditions of this trade that business historian Peter Scott, in his study of door-to-door salesmanship in interwar Britain, draws much of his evidence from *Of Love and Hunger*.[68] From an allegorical perspective, the vacuum cleaner stands for capitalism, sucking the lifeblood out of surplus youth, the "throw-outs"—as Maclaren-Ross describes them[69]—of the labour market, many of them destined to be vacuumed into the death toll of World War II.

A decade later, the Cold War of the 1950s provides the context for Greene's *Our Man in Havana*, which centres on the bathetic confusion of a vacuum cleaner with a nuclear arsenal. Allegorically, this confusion hints that the bomb is the ultimate vacuum cleaner that threatens to swallow up the world into the void. In *Nuclear Vacuum*, I propose that the historical connection between the vacuum cleaner, the never-never economy of credit, and the risk society, as well as the metaphorical connection between the vacuum and the void, contribute to the metamorphosis of the lowly vacuum cleaner into a weapon of mass destruction.

NOTES

1. See for instance Jonathan Rees, *Refrigerator*. The anthropological literature on the cooker, closely associated with the hearth, is too extensive to be listed here, but its locus classicus is Claude Lévi-Strauss, *The Raw and the Cooked* (*Le cru et le cuit*, 1964).
2. Harriette Arnow, *The Dollmaker* (1954; London: Vintage, 2017), pp. 277, 279, and *passim*.
3. See Mindy Lewis, "Abhorring a Vacuum," in *Dirt: The Quirks, Habits and Passions of Keeping House*, ed. Mindy Lewis (Berkeley, CA: Seal Press, 2009), pp. 141–50, at p. 144.
4. Kirby is a Kirby Dual Sanitronic 80 upright vacuum cleaner in the film *The Brave Little Toaster*, its deep voice provided by actor Thurl Ravenscroft. For another angry vacuum cleaner see Cora Harrison's children's book *The*

Fed-Up Vacuum Cleaner (Dublin: Mentor Books, 2002), which is dis-cussed below in the final chapter of this book.

5. Jeremy Strong, *Fatbag, the Demon Vacuum Cleaner* (1983; London: Puffin Books, 1993), pp. 42, 40.

6. See Simon Usborne, "Sucks to be him! How Henry the vacuum cleaner became an accidental design icon," based on an interview with Chris Duncan, founder of the company Numatic that produces the highly suc-cessful anthropomorphic vacuum cleaner Henry, well-known in Britain for his smiley red face and black bowler hat, in *The Guardian Weekend* (24 July 2021), pp. 21–26: https://www.theguardian.com/lifeandstyle/2021/jul/24/how-henry-vacuum-cleaner-became-accidental-design-icon. Given that Henry is notoriously inefficient and prone to pratfalls, his popu-larity among consumers can only be imputed to his goofy grin, in contrast to Sebastian's Tantalus and other monstrous vacuum cleaners. For Henry and Hetty see https://www.myhenry.com/henry-hvr160 and https://www.myhenry.com/hetty-compact-het160.

7. Jean Baudrillard, *The System of Objects* (London and New York: Verso, 1996), p. 111.

8. Ibid., p. 120.

9. See https://whitney.org/collection/works/7399.

10. Jeff Koons, quoted in caption to *New Shelton Wet/Dry Doubledecker* 1981 at MOMA https://www.moma.org/collection/works/81090.

11. https://www.periodpaper.com/products/1958-ad-laspirateur-samy-vacuum-sexual-fifties-plastic-woman-sensual-vintage-219421-ven1-274.

    The rest of the ad reads: "Aspirateur de conception révolutionnaire **tout plastique** alliant la légèreté et la robustesse … A la portée de tous par son prix le *SAMY* est **vraiment** l'aspirateur de **DEMAIN!**" In contrast to this soft-porn French ad, the American Eureka Roto-Matic promises more decorous romantic fulfilment: "Everything your heart desires—in a swivel top cleaner!" This formulation is intriguingly ambiguous: does it mean everything you could desire of a swivel top cleaner, or does the appliance itself contain everything your heart could possibly desire? The ad depicts a cylindrical machine with pink octopus-like arms extending from its swivel top, each ending in a heart-shaped bubble containing an attachment; omi-nously one of these attachments is the smiling face of the "homemaker" herself. See Ellen Lupton, *Mechanical Brides: Women and Machines from Home to Office* (New York: Smithsonian Institute, 1991), pp. 10–11. See also Rachel Dini's blog on erotic appliances: https://www.racheledini.com/post/day-and-night-the-mixmaster-is-a-delight-erotic-appliances.

12. Bob Rosenthal, *Cleaning Up New York* (New York: The Little Bookroom, 2016), p. 38. This memoir provides a rare instance in which a man, instead

of flogging vacuum cleaners to housewives, operates the machine him-self—in unconventional ways.

13. Rick Johnson and Natalie Alder, *The Vacuum Chronicles* (CreateSpace Independent Publishing Platform, 2016), kindle edition, loc. 54, 144.

14. Celestia Dew, *Seduced by the Vacuum: A Tale of Lust and Dust* (Luna Erotica, 2014).

15. B.S. Johnson, *Christie Malry's Own Double Entry* (1973; London: Picador, 2001), p. 57. Goblin was the later name of Cecil Booth's vacuum cleaner company (see Furnival, *Suck, Don't Blow*, p. 16).

16. See   https://www.poetryfoundation.org/poems/44477/ode-on-a-grecian-urn.

17. It is worth noting that James Dyson's bagless vacuum cleaners have become museum pieces, preserved as artworks rather than functional appliances. MOMA houses Dyson's Dual Cyclone Vacuum Cleaner (model DV02) 1994–95: https://www.moma.org/collection/works/88172. Likewise Dyson's DC02 De Stijl Vacuum Cleaner is housed in the Metropolitan Museum of Art, though this machine is not on view. https://www.metmuseum.org/art/collection/search/492183. Little distin-guishes Koons's "art" from Dyson's "design" apart from their creators' respective intentions.

18. Christie's records that Koons's "New Hoover Convertibles, New Shelton Wet/Drys 5-Gallon, Double Decker" realised the price of USD 11,801,000 on 13 May 2008. See https://www.christies.com/en/lot/lot-5074053.

19. See Walter Benjamin, "The Work of Art in an Age of Mechanical Reproduction" (1935), in *Illuminations*, trans. Harry Zohn, ed. Hannah Arendt (New York: Schocken Books, 1969), pp. 1–26, *passim*.

20. Ads for the Hoover Constellation are reproduced in Rachele Dini's lively blog "'Day and Night the MixMaster is a Delight': Erotic Appliances." Dini points out that the "replacement, in 1967, of the traditional house-wife of the Constellation's original print ads with a woman wearing a space suit aligned housework with intergalactic exploration, while divesting the appliance of its domestic connotations." https://www.racheledini.com/post/day-and-night-the-mixmaster-is-a-delight-erotic-appliances.

21. Freud writes, "words are frequently treated in dreams as though they were things, and for that reason they are apt to be combined in just the same way as are presentations of things." *The Interpretation of Dreams* (1900), SE 4:295–6.

22. For a reproduction see Achim Hochdorfer with Barbara Schroder, *Claes Oldenburg: The Sixties* (London: Prestel, 2012) https://bookpatrol.net/product/claes-oldenburg-the-sixties/.

23. Sigmund Freud, *Civilization and its Discontents* (1930) SE 21: 91–2.

24. William Carlos Williams, "The Red Wheelbarrow," in *Spring and All* (1923), in *The Collected Poems of William Carlos Williams*, Vol. 1: 1909–1939, ed. A. Walton Litz and Christopher MacGowan (New York: New Directions, 1991), pp. 224–225.

25. These sketches are reproduced in Barbara Haskell, *Claes Oldenburg: Object into Monument* (Pasadena Art Museum, 1971), pp. 20–21. Oldenburg explained that his monuments of quotidian objects "combine two kinds of scale—the landscape and the object—in a single space (a sheet of drawing paper)": ibid., p. 11.

26. W.H. Auden, "Musée des beaux arts," in *Collected Poems*, pp. 238–39. The poem meditates on the painting *Landscape with the Fall of Icarus* (c. 1560) attributed to Pieter Bruegel the Elder.

27. Interview with art historian and critic Ann Reynolds.

28. Quoted in Haskell, *Claes Oldenburg*, p. 20.

29. Barbara Rose, "Claes Oldenburg's Soft Machines," in Steven Henry Madoff (ed) *Pop Art: A Critical History* (Berkeley: University of California Press, 1997), pp. 228–234, at p. 231.

30. Ibid.

31. Ibid.

32. See Haskell, *Claes Oldenburg*, p. 10.

33. Ibid., p. 9.

34. Ibid.

35. Rose, "Claes Oldenburg's Soft Machines," p. 229.

36. See https://www.sevendaysvt.com/vermont/vermont-artist-recalls-life-with-claes-oldenburg-and-presents-her-own-work/Content?oid=2137810.

37. Quoted in Flavia Frigeri, *Pop Art* (New York: Thames and Hudson, 2018), p. 108.

38. See reproduction at https://museemagazine.com/culture/2018/11/12/exhibit-review-martha-rosler-irrespective.

39. See reproduction at https://www.moma.org/collection/works/150123.

40. Martha Rosler, "Place, Position, Power, Politics," in *Decoys and Disruptions: Selected Writings, 1975–2001* (Cambridge, MA: MIT Press, 2004), pp. 349–378, at pp. 353–354.

41. See reproduction at https://www.macba.cat/en/art-artists/artists/grau-eulalia/aspiradora-etnografia.

42. Ralph Ellison, Prologue to *Invisible Man* (New York: Scribners, 1952), p. 7.

43. Samuel Beckett, *Ill Seen Ill Said* (1981), in *Samuel Beckett: The Grove Centenary Edition* (New York: Grove Press, 2006), Vol. 4, pp. 451–70; at p. 470.

44. For this comparison see Leo Bersani and Ulysse Dutoit, *Arts of Impoverishment: Beckett, Rothko, Resnais* (Cambridge, MA: Harvard University Press, 1993), p. 11 and *passim*.

45. See George Washington's ledger showing a payment to "Negroes for 9 Teeth" at https://www.mountvernon.org/george-washington/health/washingtons-teeth/george-washington-and-slave-teeth/.

46. See reproduction at https://www.metmuseum.org/art/collection/search/668288 or https://www.studiomuseum.org/artworks/silence-is-golden.

47. Valerie Taber, "The Symbolism and Iconography of Kerry James Marshall's 'Silence is Golden,'" https://scalar.chapman.edu/scalar/ah-329-black-subjects-in-white-art-history-fall-2020-compendium/essays.

48. See https://www.youtube.com/watch?v=Cgn0eCtJPXA for the Ice Bag's inhalation and exhalation.

49. Karen Rosenberg, "A Low-Cost Show Re-inflates a Big Bag," *New York Times*, May 7, 2009 https://www.nytimes.com/2009/05/08/arts/design/08clae.html.

50. James Joyce, *Ulysses* (1922), ed. Hans Walter Gabler (Harmondsworth: Penguin, 1986), Ch. 11, line 1293, p. 239.

51. Two performances of Arnold's work are available on YouTube: https://www.youtube.com/watch?v=NS2-_1kWq-U; https://www.youtube.com/watch?v=6bHB3F6o3AY.

52. Luigi Russolo, *The Art of Noise*, trans. Robert Filliou (1967; Ubu Classics, 2004), p. 7; http://www.artype.de/Sammlung/pdf/russolo_noise.pdf.

53. See http://digicult.it/digimag/issue-065/the-scoppiatore-the-intona rumori-by-luigi-russolo/.

54. Edgard Varèse, "The Liberation of Sound," ed. Chou Wen-chung, *Perspectives of New Music* 5:1 (1966), pp. 11–19; at pp. 18, 14.

55. Frank Zappa, "Edgard Varèse: The Idol of My Youth," *Stereo Review* (1971), pp. 61–62; http://rchrd.com/mfom/zappa-varese.html.

56. Ibid.

57. See https://m.facebook.com/captainbeefheartandthemagicband/photos/when-i-was-a-young-man-i-was-the-best-vacuum-cleaner-salesman-in-southern-califo/1231248450345395/?_se_imp=2hi5z5fhEvykKsbut. This story, which is unattributed on Facebook, is told rather differently in Captain Beefheart's interview with Byron Coley from the January 1979 issue of *The New York Rocker*: https://web.archive.org/web/201009 18085914/http://beefheart.com/zigzag/articles/rabbit.htm. According to this 1979 account, Huxley actually bought the vacuum cleaner, an Electrolux.

58. Ibid., p. 35.

59. See image at http://www.diskant.net/features/zoot-horn-rollo/.

60. https://wiki.killuglyradio.com/wiki/File:GMVCleaner.jpg.
61. https://www.pinterest.com/pin/they-played-with-frank-zappa%2D%2D493777546616795785/.
62. https://genius.com/Frank-zappa-a-token-of-my-extreme-lyrics.
63. Lyrics to "Stick It Out," https://www.last.fm/music/Frank+Zappa/_/Stick+It+Out/+wiki.
64. See https://www.youtube.com/watch?v=5aFRBbnF-ag&t=2846s.
65. Quoted in Barry Miles, *Zappa* (New York: Grove Press, 2004), pp. 218–19.
66. Watson, "Frank Zappa's Legacy," pp. 40–1.
67. Ibid.
68. Peter Scott, *The Market Makers: Creating Mass Markets for Consumer Durables in Inter-war Britain* (Oxford: Oxford University Press, 2017), Ch. 10: 'Pushing' Vacuum Cleaners in Inter-War Britain," Oxford Scholarship Online, https://oxford-universitypressscholarship-com.proxy.uchicago.edu/view/10.1093/oso/9780198783817.001.0001/oso-9780198783817-chapter-10.
69. See Maclaren-Ross, *Selected Letters,* ed. Paul Willetts (London: Black Spring Press, 2008), p. 67.

CHAPTER 4

Nuclear Vacuum

Abstract This chapter turns to literature, focusing on two novels in which the vacuum cleaner salesman takes the leading role: Julian Maclaren-Ross's *Of Love and Hunger* (1947) and Graham Greene's *Our Man in Havana* (1958). *Of Love and Hunger* is based on the author's brief experience of selling vacuum cleaners in the bleak out-of-season seaside resort of Bognor Regis. Possibly inspired by Maclaren-Ross's inglorious profession, Greene assigns this job to the unlikely spy James Wormold in *Our Man in Havana*. This Cold War novel pivots on a comic but ominous confusion of a vacuum cleaner with a nuclear arsenal, at a time when both technologies were being promoted as defences against the Communist threat.

Keywords Julian Maclaren-Ross • Graham Greene • Espionage • Cold War • Nuclear weaponry

THE SALESMAN ONLY RINGS ONCE

Terse, hardboiled, hilarious and heart-breaking by turns, *Of Love and Hunger* is one of the neglected masterpieces of the ugly thirties. Its author Julian Maclaren-Ross, much admired in his day as a brilliant journalist, fiction-writer, parodist, and raconteur, now tends to be remembered more as a character than as an author, and more for his rackety bohemian life

© The Author(s), under exclusive license to Springer Nature
Switzerland AG 2024
M. Ellmann, *The Vacuum Cleaner*, Material Modernisms,
https://doi.org/10.1007/978-3-031-56666-0_4

than for his vivid, punchy writing—"a Dickens who had read Dashiell Hammett," as John Lehmann characterized him.[1] Maclaren-Ross features as a character, for instance, in his own best-known book *Memoirs of the Forties*,[2] a witty compendium of gossip about the London literary scene, viewed from the woozy perspective of Fitzrovia's bar stools where the author held court with the drunk and famous. As a character he also pops up in Roland Camberton's 1950 novel *Scamp*, which Maclaren-Ross attacked in a *TLS* review for "dragging in disconnectedly and to little apparent purpose a series of thinly disguised local or literary celebrities."[3] One of those celebrities, though the review doesn't mention it, is Maclaren-Ross himself, "lightly disguised as the 'former commercial traveller', Angus Sternforth Simms,"[4] who holds court in the Corney Arms from opening to closing time. "That he found time to write at all puzzled the little crowd of habitués who watched him and heard him every evening. . . . It was staggering to think of anyone writing that slick, economical prose with half a bottle of gin inside him."[5]

Anthony Powell in *A Dance to the Music of Time* casts Maclaren-Ross as X. Trapnel, the louche would-be novelist who makes a dramatic entrance in the tenth volume of the novel dressed in Maclaren-Ross's signature get-up of tropical suit, RAF greatcoat, brothel-creeper shoes, dark sunglasses, and flashy walking-stick.[6] Trapnel elopes with Kenneth Widmerpool's gorgeous wife Pamela, but she tires of her hard-up lover after a few weeks of slumming in his digs. As a parting gesture Pamela, incensed by what she regards as the incompetent conclusion of Trapnel's novel-in-progress, hurls the manuscript into the canal at Maida Vale.

Of Love and Hunger belongs to a recognizable genre of war-is-coming novels.[7] Like George Orwell's *Coming Up for Air* (1939), a better-known example of this genre, *Of Love and Hunger* is set in 1939 but wasn't published until 1947 owing to its author's truculent relations with his publishers. Notably the heroes of these interwar novels, who are also their narrators, are both traveling salesmen. Orwell's George Bowling sells insurance—which is something of an oxymoron on the eve of total war.[8] Bowling belongs to what Orwell describes as the "sinking middle-class," which is only one step above the stinking proletariat—remember Orwell's notorious pronouncement that the lower classes smell.[9] Even lower down the social ladder than George Bowling, Maclaren-Ross's hero Richard Francis Fanshawe hawks vacuum cleaners door-to-door, a job described in 1938 by a pseudonymous correspondent "A.B.C." in the *New Statesman and Nation* as "the last refuge of the man who is 'on his back' … the dregs of the employment exchanges, crooks and a lot of unhappy déclassés, ranging from gigolos to broken rubber-planters and 'unplaced' University men."[10]

Of Love and Hunger centres on a love triangle between two down-at-heels vacuum cleaner salesmen, Fanshawe and Derek Roper, and Roper's vampish wife Sukie—whose name sounds a lot like Sucko, the satirical brand-name that Maclaren-Ross assigns to Electrolux. This echo of Sucko and Sukie suggests that the vacuum cleaner, allegorically associated with capital and war, also represents the femme fatale, sucking hapless men into her fatal spell. Indeed, even the name "Roper" smacks of entanglement or "corditis." When Roper gets the sack—an inevitable fate in a business with a 500% annual labour turnover[11]—he takes a job at sea, roping in Fanshawe to look after his wife: a pretty foolproof set-up for adultery. Sure enough Fanshawe, though initially put off by Sukie's imperfect ankles, falls madly in love with her, his passion ignited when she slashes him across the knuckles with a penknife. Dogged by poverty and nosy landladies, their sado-masochistic romance quickly falls apart in a series of bathetic missed encounters. As the novel unravels, Fanshawe loses everything—his lover, his lodgings, and his dreadful job. Like Powell's X. Trapnel, he even loses his unfinished novel, forgotten in his digs when he succumbs to a recurrence of malaria, a disease he contracted in Madras in a backstory glimpsed in heated Faulknerian flashbacks.[12] Nursed back to health by Jackie Mowbray, a so-called "prospect" or potential buyer who takes a shine to this unlikely vacuum cleaner tout, Fanshawe is rescued from destitution by the outbreak of World War II. In an implausible finale, set three years after his fiasco with Sukie, Fanshawe, now engaged to Jackie, returns to Bognor in a captain's uniform and runs into his former flame. "I was thinking," he tells Sukie, "it's a damn funny world where there has to be a war before a chap gets a second chance."[13] Fanshawe has gained a second chance at chaphood not just by joining the armed forces but by casting off his castrating femme fatale, along with his subjection to the vacuum cleaner, the mechanical equivalent of a man-eating vamp—an analogy made explicit by the German company AEG in a glamorous 1929 ad for its model the "Vampyr," which features the actress Edmonde Guy as a vampirella equipped with a state-of-the-art vacuum cleaner (Fig. 4.1).

The preceding bare-bones plot-summary leaves out most of the pleasures of *Of Love and Hunger*, especially the farce of door-to-door salesmanship and the colourful band of minor characters, like the cheery conman known as Heliotrope who ends up looking forward to "a nice

Fig. 4.1 Edmonde Guy with the AEG Vampyr. AEG advertising postcard for the Vampyr vacuum cleaner. 1926. Color offset, 14.7 × 10.4 cm. Inv. PK 98/75. Photo: Sebastian Ahlers (Photo credit: bpk Bildagentur / Deutsches Historisches Museum, Berlin, Germany / Sebastian Ahlers / Art Resource, NY)

little stretch o' civvy nick."[14] Also left out is the distinctive first-person narration, which, with its slangy informality and deadpan wit, conveys the sense of being written on the hoof. Spendthrift with money, Fanshawe is tight-fisted with his grammar, omitting articles and pronouns to fashion a

staccato, telegraphic style reminiscent of Leopold Bloom's interior mono-
logue in Joyce's *Ulysses*—though Maclaren-Ross claimed to deplore
"introspection or psychological analysis" in fiction.[15]

> Three brass balls. Cool and dim inside. Dead quiet. Holy. Money changers
> in the temple. Young chap in a black coat came forward. Looked a bit like
> Ferdie [Finkelbaum], except his hair was greased down instead of kinky.[16]

Like Bloom's jerky stream-of-consciousness, Fanshawe's sentence fragments resemble newsflashes, appropriate to Fanshawe's former vocation as
a journalist as well as to the anxious pre-war atmosphere, bombarded with
apocalyptic headlines. Such headlines, along with radio announcements,
interrupt the narrative with soundbites from the wider world, including
the same newsflash about King Zog of Albania that triggers a pivotal mad-
eleine moment in Orwell's *Coming Up for Air*.[17]

In addition to this reference to Orwell, Maclaren-Ross flags his debt to
James M. Cain's *The Postman Always Rings Twice* (1934), a thriller
haunted by the trademark noir motif of damaged masculinity. In fact,
Cain's novel not only foreshadows *Of Love and Hunger* but catalyses its
adulterous plot when Sukie lends *The Postman* to Fanshawe with the ominous spoiler: "It's about a man and his mistress who plan to do away with
the woman's husband."[18] Maclaren-Ross emulates the heady mix of sex
and violence that caused Cain's novel to be banned in Boston, but *Of Love
and Hunger* stops short of murder, which would have jarred with the
novel's ironic humour.

A propos of Cain's title, Sukie asks Fanshawe:

> "How often does the salesman ring?"
> "Usually once. All he has time for."
> "Before the door's slammed on him?"
> "Exactly."[19]

This exchange accounts for Maclaren-Ross's working title for the novel,
The Salesman Only Rings Once. By amazing serendipity, a manuscript with
this title was salvaged from a dustbin by a retired removal man and presented in 2012 to Maclaren-Ross's biographer Paul Willetts, who was kind
enough to share it with me.[20] Penned in blue ink in Maclaren-Ross's tiny
meticulous handwriting, the manuscript differs from the published work
mainly in its emphasis on the salesman rather than the lover. This change

suggests that what began as an exposé of the door-to-door economy, comparable to Orwell's anthropological *The Road to Wigan Pier* (1937), morphed into a drama of obsessive love. Thus the published version introduces the soon-to-be-cuckolded Roper in the first sentence, whereas the manuscript defers his entrance for the first eight pages, focusing instead on the vacuum cleaner salesmen as they trudge through a muddy bungaloid development whose jerry-built homes flaunt names like "R Nook, Kosy Kot, Y Not: pink stucco boxes with a strip of gravel in front, each with its own garage: a desirable modern residence, hot in summer, cold in winter, £50 down."[21]

By 1942 Maclaren-Ross had come to regard *The Salesman Only Rings Once* "as a moral tale for those who think life before the war was a paradise," and he planned that the novel should culminate with the outbreak of hostilities.[22] In October 1946, after many setbacks, the author delivered his novel to Allan Wingate with the new title *Of Love and Hunger*, a phrase borrowed from the Auden and MacNeice collaboration *Letters from Iceland* (1937). "Two blokes wrote it," Fanshawe tells Jackie as he tries to remember Auden's *Letter to Lord Byron*:

> *Adventurers, though, must take things as they find them,*
> *And look for pickings where the pickings are.*
> *The drives of love and hunger are behind them*
> *Something something.*
> *Good cooking and a car.*[23]

Driven by love and hunger, Maclaren-Ross's salesmen are obliged—like vacuum cleaners—to "look for pickings where the pickings are." The brand-name "Sucko," along with its echo of Sukie, plays up the obscenity of suction while also punning on the "suckers" condemned to hawk these machines by sucking up to clients and employers and being sucked by a vampiric corporation. In this sense Sucko stands for big business as a system of sucking the lifeblood out of workers, who are caught up in the tentacles of capitalism like the "chap called Simmons" at the Sucko training session:

> Made a balls of it, getting the rake on wrong way round and then getting caught up in the hose. [Simmons] struggled about like what's-his-name in the coils of the serpent, finally cannoning into the desk and upsetting a bottle of ink.[24]

Here Fanshawe's substitution of "what's-his-name" for Laocoön makes this slapstick routine even funnier. But the scene also raises the spectre of entrapment, even strangulation by a sinister technology that crushes those whose livelihood depends upon it. Corditis indeed. The door-to-door salesman, notes ABC in *The New Statesman,* "never comes within the ambit of the commercial travellers' organization, and is mercilessly exploited."[25]

Maclaren-Ross experienced this exploitation at first hand in Bognor Regis, where he moved in 1919 with his newly married wife, a London-based actress named Elizabeth Gott. The exasperated bride left him four months later, fed up with living in the sticks in Bognor, as well as with her sybaritic husband, who expected her to do all the housework while he lounged around in a silk dressing-gown, dabbling in painting and writing. Chronically short of cash, Maclaren-Ross spotted an intriguing small ad in *The Bognor Regis Post* offering a salary of £2 a week plus commission to prospective vacuum cleaner salesmen. Together with his friend C.K. Jaeger (later the author of a whimsical vacuum cleaner novel starring the inimitable Julian himself[26]), Maclaren-Ross decided to apply, and both men were surprised to receive job offers, with the proviso that they undertake a training course at the Regional Head Office in Hove.

Here they encountered a cast of derelicts, many of them veterans of World War I, surrounded by posters exhorting them to "SAIL IN AND SELL," "DIG MORE DIRT" and "DON'T FORGET TO SMILE." A jaunty tutor in a pin-stripe suit jumped up to lead a sing-song—"I feel so happy, so happy"—followed by a pep talk promising lucrative rewards for marketing "the world's finest and most up-to-date vacuum cleaner." For the remainder of the week Maclaren-Ross and Jaeger were instructed in psychological ploys for manipulating customers, such as calling them by name and identifying with their troubles. If these strategies failed, trainees were taught the twenty-eight steps of the "Show More Dirt Demonstration," in which the salesman was to vacuum every surface of the house and dump the collected grime into a pile on the carpet.[27] Presumably the housewife, shamed by this evidence that her house was filthy, would seize the opportunity to buy a vacuum cleaner.[28]

The training programme also featured a lecture on the "Three Types of Dirt," beginning with dust and fluff, "including clinging litter," and escalating to the "most insidious enemy of all, Dangerous Destructive Germladen Grit," which could be extracted only by "the Science of Positive Agitation." This science, the lecturer concluded, "may be summed up by our slogan It Beats as It Sweeps as It Cleans,"[29] which was the refrain of the Hoover advertising jingle set to the tune of the Field Artillery March:

All the dirt, all the grit,
Hoover gets it, every bit,
For it beats, as it sweeps, as it cleans.
It deserves all its fame,
As it backs up every claim,
For it beats, as it sweeps, as it cleans.
Oh it's Hi, Hi, Hee!
The kinds of dirt are three,
We'll tell the world just what it means,
Bing! Bing! Bing!
Spring or fall, the Hoover gets them all.
For it beats, as it sweeps, as it cleans.[30]

This last line "had rhythm," Frank G. Hoover boasts in *Fabulous Dustpan*, his history of the family business. With its catchy anapaests, this refrain "rolled lightly off the tongue and it registered. It sounds simple, but it's loaded like a gun."[31] When the Hoover song was broadcast on radio in the United States, however, listeners objected to the use of a patriotic tune for advertising vacuum cleaners, and the company promptly withdrew the song from public use.[32] But it was too catchy to relinquish altogether and continued to be used to open Hoover international conventions, while the acronym of its refrain appeared on all employee service pins as "IBAISAIC."[33]

On completion of their training course, Maclaren-Ross and Jaeger were issued with company credentials, a stack of advertising flyers, and what was nicknamed a dem kit:[34] a heavy suitcase containing a vacuum-cleaner and its numerous attachments to be used for demonstration purposes. At 28 pounds, this kit was too heavy for all but the strongest (or most masochistic) women to lug around, thus excluding them from this unenviable job. Maclaren-Ross's gender-bending expedient was to wheel his dem kit around in an old pram.[35] While Electrolux employed female canvassers to arrange demonstrations in advance, rival companies, including Hoover, relied on what was called "cold knocking": a disheartening ritual in which the footsore salesman, groaning under the weight of his dem kit, would surprise the housewife on her doorstep, typically ringing only once before receiving the proverbial rebuff: "We don't want any."[36]

Armed with their dem kits, Maclaren-Ross and Jaeger set out to conquer Worthing and Brighton respectively. Conquer is the operative word,
given that salesmanship had been militarized since the late nineteenth century. Hoover even awarded "medals" to successful members of their so-
called "sales forces," similar in design to First World War medals, for
campaigns with titles like "Spring Manoeuvres," "Hoover War," and
"Hoover Crusade."[37] A rueful irony, given that many of Hoover's exploited
salesmen were down-and-out veterans of the Great War. What these
wretched functionaries had to conquer was distrust of new-fangled gim-
micks, especially those with a hefty price-tag that necessitated long-term
repayments on "the never-never plan."[38] In a typical scenario the vacuum
cleaner tout, if he succeeded in getting through the front door, would
make his pitch to a housewife whose husband was away at work, leaving
her vulnerable to a commercial seduction that verged on and sometimes
tipped over into the sexual, as it does in McCully's story discussed in the
Introduction.[39] In this "primal scene," the salesman would sweet-talk the
housewife into an infatuation with vacuum cleaner in the hope that she
could sweet-talk her husband into buying it, since married women were
legally barred from signing HP contracts. Thus, the erotic triangle in *Of
Love and Hunger* reflects the typical commercial triangle of salesman,
housewife, and absent husband.

The Salesman Only Rings Once, as its title implies, focuses on the bathos
of salesmanship rather than the merchandise itself. Maclaren-Ross shows
no interest in the vacuum cleaner as a technological innovation but only as
an allegory of the economic vacuity of Britain after World War I, sucking
vigour from its jobless, hopeless youth. The allegorical dimension of the
vacuum cleaner also prevails over its literal meaning in *Our Man in
Havana*, in which this lowly appliance is mistaken for a weapon of mass
destruction (Fig. 4.2).

THE ATOMIC PILE SUCTION CLEANER

Maclaren-Ross, in an essay titled "Excursion in Greeneland," recalls his
first meeting with Graham Greene in 1938 at a fine Queen Anne house in
Clapham, which was subsequently destroyed in the London Blitz. Like the
hapless salesmen in *Of Love and Hunger*, Maclaren-Ross only rang once
before a hostile housekeeper barred the door: "We don't want anything
today, thank you."[40] At this point Greene himself emerged and steered his
visitor to the local pub, where Maclaren-Ross admitted to his occupation:

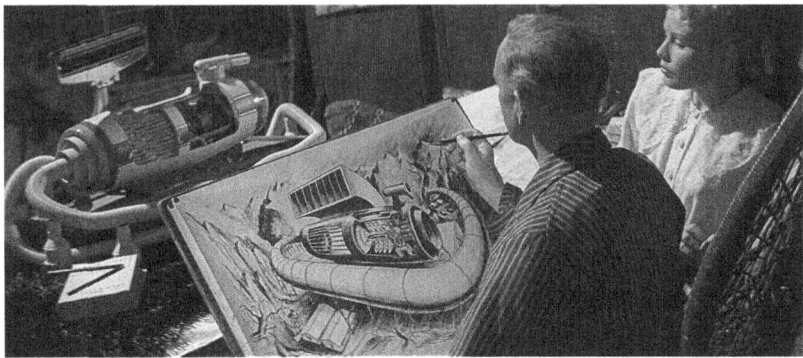

Fig. 4.2 *Our Man in Havana*, dir. Carol Reed (1959) with Alec Guinness as Jim Wormold. Columbia Pictures; Twilight Time, 2017. 1 hr., 51 min. Blu-ray Disc, 1080p HD

"I sell vacuum cleaners." Greene—unlike his housekeeper—was "plainly surprised," but confided that he once thought about signing up himself. "To write a book about it afterwards of course."

Maclaren-Ross suggests that this exchange inspired him to write the novel that became *Of Love and Hunger*.[41] But his dismal job also probably inspired Greene to cast his unlikely secret agent as a vacuum cleaner salesman in *Our Man in Havana*. This hero's name, Jim Wormold—wormy, mouldy, decadent—seems contrived to mock the virile monosyllables James Bond, the dashing secret agent recently invented by Ian Fleming, Greene's contemporary and fellow veteran of MI6. Fleming's *Dr No*, set like *Our Man in Havana* in the Caribbean and concerned with attacks on U.S. missiles, had appeared the year before Greene's parodic thriller was published in 1958. "Anxious and criss-crossed and fortyish," Wormold, who suffers from a limp, is limp in every sense compared to the glamour and machismo that Fleming attributes to agent 007.[42] Wormold also lacks Bond's sophisticated taste in cocktails: instead of vodka martinis "shaken, not stirred," Greene's hard-up hero spends his mornings boozing on daiquiris with his bibulous friend Dr Hasselbacher.

A British expat employed by Phastkleaners in louche Havana—"the great brothelley good-time city," as Greene described it[43]—Wormold devotes his meagre earnings to spoiling his beautiful teenage daughter Milly. (This daughter replaced a mistress in a former version, in Greene's effort to elude the censors.) Out of the blue the salesman finds himself solicited by Henry Hawthorne, a recruiting agent for the British Secret Service, who claims that vacuum cleaners are "an excellent cover" for a spy: "With your cleaners you've got the entrée everywhere."[44] Lured by the prospect of extra cash to pamper Milly, Wormold agrees to become Agent 59200/5.

Wormold's first ploy is to claim expenses for joining an elite country club on the pretext of making powerful contacts, but really so that Milly can go horseback-riding. Soon he is concocting spurious reports, using Lamb's *Tales from Shakespeare* as a book code, and claiming salaries for fabricated sub-agents: a trick that Greene probably borrowed from "Garbo" (Juan Pujol García, 1912–1988), the Spanish double agent loyal to Britain against Nazi Germany in World War II, who invented no fewer than twenty-six sub-agents to deceive his German handlers. Greene had learned about a similar scam when he was appointed in 1943–1944 to Kim Philby's subsection of the British Secret Service, which dealt with counter-espionage in the Iberian Peninsula. Responsible for Portugal, Greene found in this country:

> those Abwehr officers who had not been suborned already by our own service spent much of their time sending home completely erroneous reports based on information received from imaginary agents. It was a paying game, especially when expenses and bonuses were added to the cypher's salary. I had sometimes thought, in dealing with Portugal, of how easily I could have played a similar game, if I had not been content with my modest salary.[45]

In 1946 Greene incorporated this scam into a film script, which was set in Estonia in 1938 and made fun of the British Secret Service. The film was never made but the story remained in Greene's mind, "submitting itself to the wise criticism of the preconscious," until he later relocated the story to Havana, which he visited several times in the 1950s. "It struck me that here in this extraordinary city, where every vice was permissible and every trade possible, lay the true background for my comedy."[46] Greene also found that the "absurdities of the Cold War" provided a more appropriate setting for this spoof than the looming shadows of global war in 1938.[47]

At the beginning of *Our Man in Havana*, Wormold complains to Hasselbacher that Phastkleaners' new brand-name, the Atomic Pile Suction Cleaner, has frightened off his customers. Even so the company insists that "it's the best phrase anyone has thought up since 'It beats as it sweeps as it cleans.'"[48] Preposterous though it seems, this brand-name reflects the prevailing enthusiasm for nuclear power in the 1950s, despite the looming threat of nuclear annihilation. Indeed, the president of the Levy Vacuum Cleaner Company predicted that by the 1960s most homes would be cleaned by an atomic-powered vacuum cleaner.[49] The Atomic Pile Suction Cleaner later inspires Wormold's most audacious hoax when he sketches a "giant vacuum cleaner" to send to MI6, claiming that one of his agents spotted this military installation in the Oriente mountains, which was the centre of revolutionary activity in Cuba.[50] Back at Headquarters in London, the "Chief" is readily convinced that "our man in Havana" has discovered a weapon of mass destruction: "I believe we may be on to something so big that the H-bomb will become a conventional weapon."[51]

Greene's readers have been struck by the prescience of Wormold's hoax. When Shirley Hazzard suggested to the author that "the illusory 'atomic' constructions concocted by the vacuum-cleaner salesman in *Our Man in Havana* prefigured the Cuban Missile Crisis of 1962," Greene responded: "Yes. Khrushchev got that from me."[52] For today's readers, this hoax foreshadows the misinformation mustered to justify the disastrous invasion of Iraq in 2003, when Saddam Hussein was reported to be harbouring weapons of mass destruction, based on fabricated evidence provided by an Iraqi informant codenamed Curveball.[53]

In Greene's novel Wormold's imaginary sub-agents begin to take on a life of their own. "Raul," supposedly a pilot commissioned to take aerial photographs of the Oriente missile sites, turns out to have a double in real life, an aviator called Raul who is killed on his way to the airport. Stunned by this news Wormold wonders, "Can we write human beings into existence?"[54] "You talk like a novelist," replies Beatrice, the fetching spy sent from MI6 to assist the hero, who protests that Wormold treats his agents like "people in a book."[55] Christopher Hitchens has argued that this analogy between the world of espionage and that of fiction is a little too self-referential to be plausible.[56] But it offers an ominous premonition of the Iraq war in which the consequences of invented stories proved all too real.

Wormold's inventions have disastrous results, bringing Raul to life "only in order to be killed."[57] They also lead to the death of Dr. Hasselbacher and the near death of Dr. Cifuentes, a real engineer whom Wormold pretends to have recruited as a sub-agent. At the end of the novel Wormold becomes a spy for real by shooting Carter, the double-agent responsible for Hasselbacher's death. After this execution Wormold's shop is visited by a "supercilious clerk from the Consulate" who stands "stiffly among the vacuum cleaners like a disapproving tourist in a museum of phallic objects."[58] Elsewhere these machines are described as tombs and the shop as a cemetery.[59] Put together, these metaphors suggest that the vacuum cleaner showroom is a cemetery of masculinity, haunted by funerary phalloi that suck rather than shoot. By shooting Carter—which is the name of a schoolyard bully who tormented Greene as a child—Wormold graduates from sucker to avenger, and from would-be novelist to hero of his own thriller. His accession to manhood is crowned by his conquest of Beatrice, which certifies his previously questionable heterosexuality. Meanwhile the novel wavers between farce and tragedy, a contradiction ultimately resolved in satire when Wormold is summoned back to England and, instead of being hanged for treason, receives a sinecure and an OBE as a reward for keeping his mouth shut about the whole farrago.

The Atomic Pile Suction Cleaner is a grim joke on the bomb, which threatens to make a clean sweep of the planet. But this brand-name also points to the complicity between labour-saving appliances and nuclear missiles, which were developed in many cases by the same corporations.[60] Thomas Hine explains:

> Convenience in the household and defense of the homeland were linked. . . . And the association of household items with sophisticated military hardware made the weaponry somehow homier and more acceptable. Sometimes this identification of tools of war with life at home was taken to lengths that can only be called macabre, as when, soon after the explosion of the first hydrogen bomb in 1954, a newspaper ad proclaimed, "The Bomb's brilliant glow reminds me of the brilliant gleam Beacon Wax gives to floors. It's a science marvel."[61]

Not only were domestic appliances and weaponry often manufactured in the same facilities, but the appliances themselves were weaponized, along with the housewives who wielded them, in the propaganda war against Soviet Communism. A notorious instance of this weaponization was the so-called "Kitchen Debate" at the American Exhibition in Moscow in 1959 when Richard Nixon boasted to Nikita Khrushchev that American appliances made housewives' lives easier than Communism could achieve.[62] Vacuum cleaners, along with other domestic technologies, thus belong to an appliance race that provided ideological ammunition for the arms race while sugarcoating the threat of nuclear war. Greene's imaginary "Atomic

Pile Suction Cleaner" encapsulates this contradiction—a domestic gadget whose brand-name exploits the nuclear enthusiasm of the era but also marks and masks the danger of reducing the planet to a vacuum. Greene sets up a parallel between the vacuum cleaner, which is supposed to make nothing out of something, and the novelist-cum-spymaster, who contrives to make something out of nothing. More precisely, Wormold's fictions make nothing happen in a positive sense, investing nothing with the power of action. Once mobilized, however, nothing unleashes chance—Stéphane Mallarmé's *le hasard*—producing a trail of unforeseeable consequences, like the dust blown out sideways from an early vacuum cleaner. Meanwhile this appliance, rather than reducing dust to nothing, merely redistributes it; to vary Mallarmé's title, *un coup de l'aspirateur jamais n'abolira la poussière.*[63] Dust, whether in the form of fluff, clinging litter, or Dangerous Destructive Germladen Grit, marks the inevitable fallout of our efforts to control our habitat. Jean-Paul Sartre has argued that destruction is only a human experience: storms, for instance, "merely modify the distribution of masses of beings. There is no *less* after the storm than before. There is *something else.*"[64] What goes for the storm also goes for the misnamed vacuum cleaner: there is no *less* after the vacuum than before, there is *something else*—a reconfigured dustscape. There is certainly no vacuum.

NOTES

1. John Lehmann and Phillip Fry, "An Interview in Austin with John Lehmann," *Studies in the Novel* 3:1 (1971) 80–96; at p. 92.
2. Maclaren-Ross, *Memoirs of the Forties* (1965), in *Collected Memoirs* (London: Black Spring Press, 2001).
3. Maclaren-Ross, "Cosmopolitan Characters," review of Aubrey Menen, *The Backward Bride* and Roland Camberton, *Scamp*, *Times Literary Supplement* 2545 (10 November 1950) 705.
4. Iain Sinclair, "Man in a Macintosh: Roland Camberton, the Great Invisible of English Fiction," introduction to Roland Camberton, *Scamp* (1950; Nottingham: New London Editions, 2010), pp. 5–18, at p.7. See also David Herman, "A Lost Generation: Roland Camberton at 100," *Times Literary Supplement* 6165 (28 May 2021) 21.
5. Camberton, *Scamp*, p. 36.
6. Anthony Powell, *Books Do Furnish a Room* (1971), Book 10 of *A Dance to the Music of Time* (Chicago: University of Chicago Press, 2010), esp. pp. 105–6.

7. See D.J. Taylor, introduction to Julian Maclaren-Ross, *Of Love and Hunger*, p. xi; see also Gill Plain, *Women's Fiction of the Second World War: Gender, Power, and Resistance* (New York: St. Martin's Press, 1996), p. 38.

8. Orwell wrote to John Sceats, an ILP member and insurance salesman, asking for details of the life of a rep, because he wanted a plausible job for a "£5 a week and a house in the suburbs" man who would have the opportunity of driving around a bit and could be pictured as "slightly bookish." As Bernard Crick comments in his biography of Orwell, "This was the birth of George Bowling." Crick, *George Orwell: A Life* (Harmondsworth: Penguin, 1980), p. 370.

9. George Orwell, *The Road to Wigan Pier* (New York: Harcourt Brace and World, 1958), pp. 172–174, 97. Bowling belongs to what Ross McKibben (*Classes and Cultures* [Oxford: Oxford University Press, 1998], p. 45) describes as "the world of petty clerks and salesmen, insurance agents and shop assistants, the world of H.G. Wells's 'Kipps' which gave English life its particular cast." Socially marginal, this group was "often of immediate working-class origin, often deeply alienated from its work—more alienated, perhaps, than any other social group." See also John Sutherland, *Orwell's Nose: A Pathological Biography* (London; Reaktion, 2016), Appendix III: "The Smell Narrative of *The Road to Wigan Pier*,"pp. 240–1. Although lower down the salesmen's pecking order, Fanshawe has fallen from a higher rung of the social ladder: a genteel down-and-out.

10. A.B.C., "Sales Representative," pp. 863–864. While Bowling sells insurance, a vacuum cleaner salesman makes a cameo appearance in Orwell's *Keep the Aspidistra Flying*, p. 29: "On the second floor [of the boarding house] lived Lorenheim, a dark, meagre, lizard like creature of uncertain age and race, who made about thirty-five shillings a week by touting vacuum-cleaners. ... Lorenheim was one of those people who have not a single friend in the world and who are devoured by a lust for company." Devoured and devouring, he pounces on anyone who passes by his room and sucks them in, like the appliance that he tries to sell.

11. Scott, "Managing Door-to-Door Sales of Vacuum Cleaners in Interwar Britain," p. 773.

12. Fanshawe's implied dark past in Madras harks back to Julian Maclaren-Ross's short story, "A Bit of a Smash in Madras," which he submitted to Cyril Connolly for publication in *Horizon* in 1939. For the full amusing story see Maclaren-Ross, *Collected Memoirs*, pp. 230–1; see also Paul Willetts, *Fear and Loathing in Fitzrovia: The Bizarre Life of Writer, Actor, Soho Dandy Julian Maclaren-Ross* (Stockport: Dewi Lewis Publishing, 2003), p. 81. Maclaren-Ross writes admiringly of William Faulkner's *The Sound and the Fury* in "A Saga of the Deep South" and parodies Faulkner brilliantly in "A Cable"; see Maclaren-Ross, *Bitten by the Tarantula and*

Other Writing (London: Black Spring Press, 2005), pp. 326–331 and 485–488.

13. *Of Love and Hunger*, p. 203. See Maclaren-Ross, *Selected Letters*, p. 67: "the idea being that it takes a war for the throw-outs to get back into their former position in life."

14. *Of Love and Hunger*, p. 196.

15. In a letter to Dan Davin of 18 January 1953 Maclaren-Ross mentions his plan (never to be fulfilled) to write a book of critical essays on "a few authors who've either not been mentioned enough or, in my opinion, not examined in the way they should be—the connecting link being the fact that they show their characters in action rather than through introspection or psychological analysis": Maclaren-Ross, *Selected Letters*, p. 142; see also Willetts, *Fear and Loathing*, p. 238. In 1942, when Maclaren-Ross was posted by the British Army in Southend-on-Sea, he wrote to Rupert Hart-Davis to ask for a copy of Joyce's *Ulysses* (ibid., p. 32).

16. Ibid., p. 37. In *Of Love and Hunger,* the vacuum cleaner business is dominated by Jews, a feature even more pronounced in the manuscript, which suggests that Maclaren-Ross toned down these hints of antisemitism after World War II.

17. George Orwell, *Coming Up for Air*, p. 31.

18. Ibid., p. 59.

19. Maclaren-Ross, *Of Love and Hunger*, p. 59.

20. See Paul Willetts, Afterword to the German edition of Julian Maclaren-Ross's novel *Of Love and Hunger:* https://www.paulwilletts.com/2532807-of-love-and-hunger.

21. Manuscript of *The Salesman Only Rings Once*, p. 18.

22. Maclaren-Ross, *Selected Letters*, pp. 66–7.

23. W. H. Auden, "Letter to Lord Byron" II, in Auden and Louis MacNeice, *Letters from Iceland*, in W.H. Auden, *Collected Poems*, ed. Edward Mendelson, 2 vols. (Princeton: Princeton University Press, 2022), Vol. 1, pp. 227–60; at p. 237. The forgotten lines are "They can't afford to be particular: / And those who like good cooking and a car...." A fuller quotation appears as the epigraph to *Of Love and Hunger,* Part II, p. 53.

24. *Of Love and Hunger*, p. 96.

25. A.B.C., "Sales Representative," p. 864.

26. C.K. Jaeger, *The Man in the Top Hat* (London: Grey Walls Press, 1949).

27. This sales technique apparently goes back to the days of carpet sweepers when Melville Bissell, who obtained his first patent for a carpet sweeper in 1876, demonstrated its effectiveness by throwing a handful of street dirt on carpets. Known as the Bissell Centre Bearing Sweeper, this machine was said to be "the first sweeper that picked up more dust than it managed to

stir up" (Gantz, *The Vacuum* Cleaner, p. 30). In McCully's story "How's Your Vacuum Cleaner Working?" (p. 29), the elder salesman "actually produces a bag of dirt and strews it on the floor" to show how the nozzle "glops up the sand and dirt."

28. *Of Love and Hunger*, p. 17; Willetts, *Fear and Loathing*, pp. 60–62.
29. Maclaren-Ross, *Collected Memoirs*, p. 186.
30. Gantz, *The Vacuum Cleaner*, p. 90. Note that the racist Hoover ad featuring two black maids, which is discussed in the Introduction, varies this jingle: "It *LIGHTS* as it *BEATS* as it *SWEEPS* as it *CLEANS*." https://i.ebayimg.com/images/g/fcMAAOSwb0Bd9rPM/s-l640.jpg.
31. Hoover, *Fabulous Dustpan*, p. 128.
32. Ibid., p. 143.
33. Gantz, *The Vacuum Cleaner*, p. 90.
34. Willetts, *Fear and Loathing*, p. 62.
35. Ibid., p. 63. In John Cheever's *The Wapshot Chronicle* (1957; London: Vintage Digital, 2010), a young housewife visited by a vacuum cleaner salesman sympathizes with his load: "I imagine you must get tired and footsore going around with that heavy bag all day long" (p. 229).
36. See Peter Scott, *The Market Makers*, p. 245; Glen Shelton, *The Complete Guide to Door-to-Door Cold Knocking* (2016) http://www.leadheroes.com/the-complete-guide-to-door-to-door-cold-knocking/.
37. Peter Scott, "Managing Door-to-Door Sales," p. 780. See also Timothy B. Spears, *100 Years on the Road*, p. 208.
38. See Peter Scott, "The Twilight World of Interwar British Hire Purchase," *passim*.
39. In the film *The Green Man* the vacuum cleaner salesman succeeds in poaching the housewife from her stodgy fiancé.
40. Maclaren-Ross, "Excursion in Greeneland," *Collected Memoirs*, pp. 194–206; at p. 194.
41. A more likely story was that Maclaren-Ross was competing with his friend and fellow salesman C.K. "Mac" Jaeger to write a novel about vacuum cleaner salesmen. According to Willetts (*Fear and Loathing*, p. 63): "When Mac announced that he planned to write something about door-to-door salesmen, his friend was indignant. 'Me too,' Julian said. 'And *I'm* going to do it first....'" He beat Jaeger by two years: Jaeger's fantasy novel *The Man in the Top Hat*, which focuses on the tyrannical figure of "Uncle Julian," was published in 1949, two years after *Of Love and Hunger*.
42. Graham Greene, *Our Man in Havana* (1958; New York: Penguin, 2007), p. 4.
43. Graham Greene, *Reflections*, ed. Judith Adamson (London: Vintage, 2014), p. 285.

44. Greene, *Our Man in Havana*, p. 25.
45. Graham Greene, *Ways of Escape* (1980; London: Vintage, 2002), p. 238–39.
46. Ibid., p. 240.
47. Peter Hulme, "Graham Greene and Cuba: Our Man in Havana?" *New West Indian Guide*, 82:3/4 (2008) 185–209; at pp. 187–88.
48. *Our Man in Havana*, p. 6. Overshadowed by the threat of nuclear annihilation, the 1950s also gave rise to a bizarre optimism about the beneficial possibilities of nuclear energy. In *Our Man in Havana*, Phastcleaner's Atomic Pile Suction Cleaner parodies this fad for nuclear chic. The Doomsday scenario and nuclear-powered mod cons come together in Ray Bradbury's classic short story "There Will Come Soft Rains," discussed below in the Coda of this book.
49. Donald E. Morse, in "Sterile Men and Nuclear-Powered Vacuum Cleaners: The Atom Bomb and Atomic Energy in 1950s American Science Fiction," in Donald E. Morse (ed) *Anatomy of Science Fiction* (Newcastle: Cambridge Scholars Press, 2006), pp. 83–94; at p. 87.
50. Greene, *Our Man in Havana*, p. 81; Hulme, "Graham Greene and Cuba," p. 194.
51. Greene, *Our Man in Havana*, p. 81.
52. Shirley Hazzard, *Greene on Capri: A Memoir* (London: Virago, 2000), p. 26.
53. See Christopher Hull, *Our Man Down in Havana: The Story Behind Graham Greene's Cold War Spy Novel* (New York and London: Pegasus Books, 2019), p. 289.
54. Greene, *Our Man in Havana*, p. 121.
55. Ibid., p. 112.
56. Christopher Hitchens, "Death From a Salesman: Graham Green's Bottled Ontology," in Greene, *Our Man in Havana*, p. xvii.
57. Greene, *Our Man in Havana*, p. 124.
58. Ibid., p. 212.
59. Ibid., pp. 121, 142.
60. Thomas Hine, *Populuxe* (New York: MJF Books, 1999), p.128.
61. Ibid., pp. 128–29.
62. See Sarah T. Phillips and Shane Hamilton, *The Kitchen Debate and Cold War Consumer Politics* (Boston, MA and New York: Bedford/St. Martin's, 2014); Joy Parr, "Modern Kitchen, Good Home, Strong Nation," *Technology and Culture* 434 (2004) 657–67; Dini, *"All-Electric" Narratives*, pp. 9, 19, 54–56, 157.

63. Stéphane Mallarmé, *Un coup de dés jamais n'abolira le hasard* (A throw of the dice will never abolish chance) 1897/1914. https://www.poetryin-translation.com/PITBR/French/MallarmeUnCoupdeDes.php. By playing on the title of this famous poem I'm suggesting that dust is equivalent to chance (*le hasard*), unpredictable and irrepressible. Dust resembles Derrida's concept of the trace, the residue of absence that inter-rupts and destabilizes presence.

64. Jean-Paul Sartre, *Being and Nothingness: An Essay on Phenomenological Ontology*, trans. Hazel E. Barnes (1943; New York: Philosophical Library, 1956), pp. 8–9.

CHAPTER 5

Coda: The House Was Clean

Abstract This coda reviews the ways in which the vacuum cleaner has been anthropomorphized, sexualized, and demonized in art and popular culture. As these protean transformations indicate, the vacuum cleaner's cultural meanings greatly exceed its workaday function. In psychoanalyst Melanie Klein's terminology, the vacuum cleaner has come to represent the "bad breast," imagined as a nagging harpy, bloodsucking vampire, or man-eating monster.

Keywords Anthropomorphosis • Melanie Klein • Ray Bradbury

In exploring the cultural history of the vacuum cleaner, this book has attempted to unite the approaches of the collector and the allegorist, in Walter Benjamin's terms. From the collector's point of view, the vacuum cleaner functions as a metonym for the twentieth-century domestic revolution. From the allegorist's point of view, the vacuum serves a metaphor for the emptiness of progress. Typically brandished by a chic smiling housewife in mid-century advertising, this iconic appliance connotes modernity as sleek efficiency. The reality, of course, differs drastically from the hype. Clumsy, noisy, prone to mishaps like the broken belt in Fanshawe's hapless demonstration, this cumbersome machine has increased the household labour it purports to "save."

© The Author(s), under exclusive license to Springer Nature Switzerland AG 2024
M. Ellmann, *The Vacuum Cleaner*, Material Modernisms,
https://doi.org/10.1007/978-3-031-56666-0_5

Hence the vacuum cleaner has inspired fear and loathing that contradicts its space-age fanfare. Figured as a "monster" in Anna Sebastian's 1944 novel of that name, Tantalus the vacuum cleaner is a fascist dictator hell-bent to swallow up the world. Elsewhere the vacuum cleaner is depicted as a vampire or a cannibal, as in Grau's *Aspiradora*: a cannibal that devours those "little bits of ourselves" we leave behind, as Aubrey Bell the salesman describes this detritus in Carver's "Collectors." As a matter of fact, 75–80% of vacuum cleaner litter consists of human skin cells.[1] Portrayed as a flesh-eating, blood-drinking ogre, like the Kleinian bad breast, the vacuum cleaner also morphs into a furious Kleinian baby. In Cora Harrison's children's book *The Fed-Up Vacuum Cleaner*, the eponymous appliance spits out refuse instead of sucking it up, strewing spiders all over the carpet. Its tantrum spent, the "little vacuum cleaner" returns to its "reparative" activities, cleaning up the wreckage of its paranoid-schizoid frenzy, to be rewarded with a sibling in the form of an electric floor cleaner.[2]

Above all, the vacuum cleaner is anthropomorphic, whether in the guise of a roaring Hitler (Sebastian's *The Monster*), an avuncular curmudgeon (Kirby in *The Brave Little Toaster*), a baby in the throes of anal sadism (Harrison's fed-up vacuum cleaner), a crazed proletarian revolutionary (*Fatbag*), or a seductive siren (*The Vacuum Chronicles*). When it's not on a rampage, the vacuum cleaner is depicted as a buffoon, accident-prone and histrionic. Rather than gliding smoothly over carpets and upholstery, it trips and stumbles, belching and hiccupping on dirt instead of swallowing it politely. As a sexual partner it rarely lives up to its deep-throated promise: "it doesn't go anywhere," Bob Rosenthal laments.

Breathing and sucking, swelling and detumescing, lurching and tumbling, crashing and thundering, the vacuum cleaner shows an animation that other appliances can scarcely emulate. But it's a graceless animation, funny for reasons that Henri Bergson adduces in his famous essay on "Laughter": "The laughable element … consists of a certain MECHANICAL INELASTICITY, just where one would expect to find the wide-awake adaptability and the living pliableness of a human being."[3] The vacuum cleaner is funny because it fails to behave like a human being (though few humans are as pliable as Bergson presumes)—but to expect such behaviour from a machine is even funnier. This appliance both invites and frustrates the anthropomorphic impulse to vacuum the otherness out of the object world by sucking everything into the human. Funny though it is, the vacuum cleaner also inspires the dread that culminates in *Our Man in Havana* when this appliance is depicted as a nuclear weapon. Although there is no vacuum in a vacuum cleaner, this misnomer augurs an annihilation so complete that even dust—which never goes away—would be eradicated: a "remainderless cataclysm," in Jacques Derrida's words, which entails "the absolute effacement of any possible trace."[4] Meanwhile the fantasy of dustlessness, which has driven the technological development of the vacuum cleaner as well as its adoption by house-proud consumers, brings with it the "manufactured risk" of allergies and compromised immunity.

Modernity aspires to a dust-free world, cleansed of the detritus of history: those "bits of ourselves" and our antecedents that bind us to the past. "The New," as Koons titles his vacuum cleaner installation, celebrates (or satirises) the extinction of the old in a future disinfected of the past. Facing this antiseptic future, some might sympathise with Arnold Bennett's skinflint Henry Earlforward in *Riceyman Steps*, cited in the Introduction to this book. Miserly even about his dust, Earlforward objects to its removal by the vacuum cleaner company. "He could not like the cleanliness. He had been robbed of something. And the place had lost its look of home; it was bare, inhospitable, and he was a stranger in it."[5] This home has itself become a vacuum, robbed of the dusty accumulations of the past.

My study has emphasized the fraudulence of the vacuum cleaner, its broken promises to save time and labour as well as to eliminate the dust that never goes away. Whatever its shortcomings, however, the vacuum cleaner is here to stay, as stubborn as the dust it fails to conquer. Moreover, this appliance continues to evolve, dispensing with "corditis" and other inconveniences in models like the bagless cordless Dyson and the robotic Roomba. Its automatism looks forward to a future when homes will clean themselves, as in Ray Bradbury's story "There Will Come Soft Rains" (1950), in which an army of robots continues to vacuum the house after its owners have been incinerated by a nuclear bomb:

Nine-fifteen, sang the clock, *time to clean.*
   Out of warrens in the wall, tiny robot mice darted. The rooms were acrawl with the small cleaning animals, all rubber and metal. They thudded against chairs, whirling their mustached runners, kneading the rug nap, sucking gently at hidden dust. Then, like mysterious invaders, they popped into their burrows. Their pink electric eyes faded. The house was clean.[6]

NOTES

1. See Virginia Smith, *Clean: A History of Personal Hygiene and Purity* (Oxford and New York: Oxford University Press, 2007), p. 11.

2. See Melanie Klein, "Notes on some schizoid mechanisms," *International Journal of Psycho-Analysis* 27 (1946), 99–110. In Cora Harrison's *The Fed-Up Vacuum Cleaner*, it's worth noting that the father joins the "little vacuum cleaner" in cleaning up the house, his intervention enabling the reparative work that Klein associates with the depressive position, in which the "good breast" and the "bad breast" are reintegrated, as opposed to the paranoid-schizoid position in which they are split in two. Harrison's Kleinian parable bears comparison to Maurice Ravel's operetta *L'enfant et les sortilèges* (1925), with its libretto by Colette, in which a child takes revenge against his mother by attacking household objects that attack him in return. Klein, basing her remarks on a review rather than the operetta itself, interpreted it as a demonstration of her theories of paranoia and reparation; see Melanie Klein, "Infantile Anxiety-Situations Reflected in a Work of Art and in the Creative Impulse," *International Journal of Psycho-Analysis* 10 (1929) 436–443.

3. Henri Bergson, *Laughter: An Essay on the Meaning of the Comic* (1900), trans. Cloudesley Brereton and Fred Rothwell (1911) https://www.gutenberg.org/files/4352/4352-h/4352-h.htm

4. Jacques Derrida, "No Apocalypse, Not Now (Full Speed Ahead, Seven Missiles, Seven Missives)," trans. Catherine Porter and Philip Lewis, *Diacritics* 14:2 (1984) 20–31; at pp. 21, 28.

5. Bennett, *Riceyman Steps*, p. 54.

6. Ray Bradbury, "August 2057: There Will Come Soft Rains," *The Martian Chronicles* (New York: Harper Collins, 2011), pp.248–56; at p. 249. This short story first appeared in the 6 May 1950 issue of *Collier's Weekly* and was revised and included as a chapter titled "August 2026: There Will Come Soft Rains" in Bradbury's *The Martian Chronicles* that was also first published in May 1950. The 1997 edition of *The Martian Chronicles* advanced all dates in the 1950 edition by 31 years, changing the title to "August 2057: There Will Come Soft Rains."

BIBLIOGRAPHY

A.B.C. "Sales Representative." *The New Statesman and Nation* N.S. 15:378 (21 May 1938) 863–865.

Adam, Ruth. *A Woman's Place, 1910–1975.* New York: Norton, 1975.

Appadurai, Arjun (ed). *The Social Life of Things: Commodities in Cultural Perspective.* Cambridge: Cambridge University Press, 1986.

Arnow, Harriette. *The Dollmaker.* 1954; London: Vintage, 2017.

Auden, W.H. "Musée des beaux arts." 1939. In Auden, W.H. *Collected Poems.* Ed. Edward Mendelson. 2 vols. Princeton: Princeton University Press, 2022, Vol. 1, pp. 338-9.

Auden, W.H. and Louis MacNeice. *Letters from Iceland.* 1937. *Collected Poems,* Vol. 1, pp. 227–89.

Barthes, Roland. "The Reality Effect" (1975). In *The Rustle of Language.* Trans. Richard Howard. Berkeley: University of California Press, 1989, pp. 141–148.

Baudrillard, Jean. *The System of Objects.* London and New York: Verso, 1996.

Beauvoir, Simone de. *The Second Sex* (1952). Trans. H.M. Parshley. New York: Vintage Books, 1989.

Beck, Ulrich. "Politics of Risk Society." In Franklin, Jane (ed). *The Politics of Risk Society,* pp. 9–22.

Beckett, Samuel. *Ill Seen Ill Said.* 1981. In *Samuel Beckett: The Grove Centenary Edition.* New York: Grove Press, 2006. Vol. 4, pp. 451–70.

Benjamin, Walter. *Paris: The Capital of the Nineteenth* Century. In *Selected Writings.* Vol. 3. Ed. Howard Eiland and Michael W. Jennings. Cambridge, MA and London: Belknap Press of Harvard University Press, 2002, pp. 32–49.

© The Author(s), under exclusive license to Springer Nature   105
Switzerland AG 2024
M. Ellmann, *The Vacuum Cleaner,* Material Modernisms,
https://doi.org/10.1007/978-3-031-56666-0

———. *The Arcades Project.* Ed. Rolf Tiedemann. Trans. Howard Eiland and Kevin McLaughlin. Cambridge, MA: Harvard University Press, 1999.

———. "The Work of Art in an Age of Mechanical Reproduction." 1935. In *Illuminations.* Trans. Harry Zohn. Ed. Hannah Arendt. New York: Schocken Books, 1969, pp. 1–26.

Bennett, Arnold. *Riceyman Steps.* 1923; London: Penguin, 2016.

Bennett, Jane. *Vibrant Matter.* Durham, NC: Duke University Press, 2010.

Benson, John and Laura Ugolini (eds). *Cultures of Selling: Perspectives on Consumption and Society since 1700.* Aldershot, Hants.: Ashgate, 2006.

Berger, Arthur Asa. *The Objects of our Affection: Semiotics and Consumer Culture.* New York: Palgrave Macmillan, 2020.

Bergson, Henri. *Laughter: An Essay on the Meaning of the Comic.* 1900. Trans. Cloudesley Brereton and Fred Rothwell. 1911. https://www.gutenberg.org/files/4352/4352-h/4352-h.htm

Bersani, Leo and Ulysse Dutoit. *Arts of Impoverishment: Beckett, Rothko, Resnais.* Cambridge, MA: Harvard University Press, 1993.

Bezeczky, Gábor. "Literal Language." *New Literary History* 22:3 (1991) 603–611.

Bittman, Michael, James Mahmud Rice, and Judy Waczman. "Appliances and their Impact: The ownership of domestic technology and time spent on household work." *British Journal of Sociology* 55:3 (2004) 401–423.

Booth, H. Cecil. "The Origin of the Vacuum Cleaner." *Transactions of the Newcomen Society* 15:1 (1934) 85-98.

Bose, Christine E., Philip L. Bereano, and Mary Molloy. "Household Technology and the Social Construction of Housework." *Technology and Culture* 25 (January 1984) 53–82.

Bowden, Sue and Avner Offer. "Household Appliances and the Use of Time: The United States and Britain since the 1920s." *The Economic History Review*, New Series 47:4 (1994) 725–748.

Bowden, Sue. "The technological revolution that never was: Gender, class and the diffusion of household appliances in interwar England." In V. de Grazia and E. Furlough (eds). *The Sex of Things: Gender and Consumption in Historical Perspective.* Berkeley: University of California Press, 1996, pp. 244–74.

Bowen, Elizabeth. *The Hotel.* 1927; Chicago: University of Chicago Press, 2012.

Bradbury, Ray. "August 2057: There Will Come Soft Rains." In *The Martian Chronicles.* New York: Harper Collins, 2011, pp. 248–56.

Brown, Bill. "Thing Theory." *Critical Inquiry* 28 (2001) 1–22.

——— *A Sense of Things: The Object Matter of American Literature.* Chicago: University of Chicago Press, 2003.

——— "Reification, Reanimation and the American Uncanny." *Critical Inquiry* 32 (2006) 175–207.

——— *Other Things.* Chicago: University of Chicago Press, 2015.

Camberton, Roland. *Scamp.* 1950; Nottingham: New London Editions, 2010.

Carver, Raymond. "Collectors." In *Will You Please be Quiet, Please?* New York: Random House, 1992, pp. 102–110.

—— "Put Yourself in My Shoes." 1972. In *Will You Please be Quiet, Please?*, pp. 97–110.

—— "On Writing." In *Fires: Essays, Poems, Stories.* London: Collins Harvill, 1985, pp. 22–27.

Cheever, John. *The Wapshot Chronicle.* 1957; London: Vintage Digital, 2010.

—— *The Wapshot Scandal.* 1959; London: Vintage, 1998.

Cockburn, Cynthia and Ruža First-Dilić. *Bringing Technology Home: Gender and technology in a changing Europe.* Buckingham: Open University Press, 1994.

Conradi, Raymond. *Iris Murdoch: A Life.* New York and London: Harper Collins, 2001.

Corker, Le'Tonda. *Oh Noooooo! The Washing Machine Ate my Socks.* Kindle, 2021.

Cowan, Ruth Schwarz. *More Work for Mother: The Ironies of Household Technology from the Open Hearth to the Microwave.* New York: Basic Books, 1983.

Cox, Rosie. "Dishing the Dirt: Dirt in the Home." In *Dirt: The Filthy Reality of Everyday Life.* London: Profile Books, 2011, pp. 37–74.

Crick, Bernard. *George Orwell: A Life.* Harmondsworth: Penguin, 1980.

Csikszentmihalyi, Mihaly, and Eugene Rochberg-Halton. *The Meaning of Things: Domestic Symbols and the Self.* Cambridge and New York: Cambridge University Press, 1981.

Davidson, Caroline. *A Woman's Work is Never Done: A History of Housework in the British Isles 1650–1950.* London: Chatto and Windus, 1952.

Derrida, Jacques. "No Apocalypse, Not Now Full Speed Ahead, Seven Missiles, Seven Missives." Trans. Catherine Porter and Philip Lewis. *Diacritics* 14:2 (1984) 20–31.

Dew, Celestia. *Seduced by the Vacuum: A Tale of Lust and Dust.* Luna Erotica, 2014.

Dini, Rachel. *"All-Electric" Narratives: Time-Saving Appliances and Domesticity in American Literature, 1945–2020.* New York: Bloomsbury Academic, 2021.

Disch, Thomas M. *The Brave Little Toaster.* 1980; New York: Doubleday, 1986.

Douglas, Mary. *Purity and Danger.* 1966; London: Routledge, 2002.

Edwards, Clive. "Buy Now—Pay Later. Credit: The Mainstay of the Retail Furniture Business?" In Benson, John and Laura Ugolini (eds) *Cultures of Selling*, pp. 127–52.

Edwards, Kevin and Pia Ostensson. "'The Man Who Vacuum Cleaned the Atlantic': The aerosol collector and Gunnar Erdtman's attempts to measure pollen rain." *Palynology* 48:1 (2023). https://doi.org/10.1080/01916122.2023.2260437

Ellison, Ralph. *Invisible Man.* New York: Scribners, 1952.

Ellmann, Mary. *Thinking About Women.* New York: Harcourt, Brace & World, 1968.

Forty, Adrian. *Objects of Desire: Design and Society from Wedgwood to IBM.* New York: Pantheon, 1986.

Franklin, Jane (ed). *The Politics of Risk Society*. Cambridge, UK and Malden, MA: Polity Press, 1998.

Freedgood, Elaine. *The Ideas in Things: Fugitive Meaning in the Victorian Novel*. Chicago: University of Chicago Press, 2006.

Fremlin, Celia. *The Seven Chars of Chelsea*. London: Methuen, 1940.

Freud, Sigmund. *The Standard Edition of the Complete Psychological Works of Sigmund Freud*. Trans. James Strachey. 24 vols. London: Hogarth Press, 1953–1974. Cited as SE.

——— *The Interpretation of Dreams*. 1900. SE 4 and 5: ix-627.

——— "Jokes and their Relation to the Unconscious." 1905. SE 8:97–102.

——— "The Antithetical Meaning of Primal Words." 1910. SE 11:153–162.

——— "The 'Uncanny'" 1919. SE 17:217–256.

——— *Civilization and its Discontents*. 1930. SE 21: 57–146.

Frigeri, Flavia. *Pop Art*. New York: Thames and Hudson, 2018.

Furnival, Jane. *Suck, Don't Blow: The Gripping Story of the Vacuum Cleaner and Other Labour Saving Machines Around the House*. London: Michael O'Mara Books, 1998.

Gantz, Carroll. *The Vacuum Cleaner: A History*. Jefferson, NC and London: McFarland & Co., 2012.

Gardiner, Juliet. *The Thirties: An Intimate History*. London: HarperPress, 2010.

Giddens, Anthony. *The Nation-State and Violence*. Vol. 2 of *A Contemporary Critique of Historical Materialism*. Berkeley: University of California Press, 1981.

Giddens, Anthony and Christopher Pierson. *Conversations with Anthony Giddens: Making Sense of Modernity*. Stanford, CA: Stanford University Press, 1998.

——— "Risk and Responsibility." *The Modern Law Review* 62:1 (1999) 1–10.

Giles, Judy. *The Parlour and the Suburb: Domestic Identities, Class, Femininity and Modernity*. Oxford and New York: Berg, 2004.

Greene, Graham. *Our Man in Havana*. 1958; New York: Penguin, 2007.

——— *Ways of Escape*. 1980; London: Vintage, 2002.

——— Reflections. Ed. Judith Adamson. London: Vintage, 2014.

Greenfield, Adam. "Labour-saving technology and the ideology of ease." In Steierhoffer, Eszter and Justin McGuirk (eds). *Home Futures: Living in Yesterday's Tomorrow*. London: Design Museum Publishing, 2018, pp. 265–73.

Greenfield, Jill and Chris Reid. "Women's Magazines and the Commercial Orchestration of Femininity in the 1930s: Evidence from *Women's Own*." *Media History* 4:2 (1998) 161–74.

Hardyment, Christina. *From Mangle to Microwave: The mechanization of household work*. Cambridge, UK: Polity Press, 1988.

Harrison, Cora. *The Fed-Up Vacuum Cleaner*. Dublin: Mentor Books, 2002.

Haskell, Barbara. *Claes Oldenburg: Object into Monument*. Pasadena, CA: Pasadena Art Museum, 1971.

Hazzard, Shirley. *Greene on Capri: A Memoir.* London: Virago, 2000.

Herman, David. "A Lost Generation: Roland Camberton at 100." *Times Literary Supplement* 6165 (28 May 2021) 21.

Hine, Thomas. *Populuxe.* New York: MJF Books, 1999.

Holmes, Hannah. *The Secret Life of Dust: From the cosmos to the kitchen counter, the big consequences of little things.* New York: Wiley, 2001.

Horsfield, Margaret. *Biting the Dust: The Joys of Housework.* London: Fourth Estate, 1997.

Hoover, Frank. *Fabulous Dustpan: The Story of the Hoover.* Cleveland and New York: The World Publishing Company, 1955.

Hoy, Suellen M. *Chasing Dirt: The American Pursuit of Cleanliness.* New York: Oxford University Press, 1995.

Hull, Christopher. *Our Man Down in Havana: The Story Behind Graham Greene's Cold War Spy Novel.* New York and London: Pegasus Books, 2019.

Hulme, Peter. "Graham Greene and Cuba: Our Man in Havana?" *New West Indian Guide* 82:3/4 (2008) 185–209.

Jaeger, C.K. *The Man in the Top Hat.* London: Grey Walls Press, 1949.

James, Henry. Preface to the New York Edition of *Roderick Hudson.* 1907. Ed. Geoffrey Moore. London: Penguin, 1986.

Johnson, B.S. *Christie Malry's Own Double Entry.* 1973; London: Picador, 2001.

Johnson, Paul. *Saving and Spending: The Working-class Economy in Britain 1870–1939.* Oxford: Clarendon Press, 1985.

Johnson, Rick and Natalie Alder. *The Vacuum Chronicles.* CreateSpace Independent Publishing Platform, 2016, kindle edition.

Joyce, James. *Ulysses.* 1922. Ed. Hans Walter Gabler. Harmondsworth: Penguin, 1986.

Kee, Robert. *The World We Left Behind: A Chronicle of the Year 1939.* London: Weidenfeld and Nicholson, 1984.

Klein, Melanie. "Infantile Anxiety-Situations Reflected in a Work of Art and in the Creative Impulse." *International Journal of Psychoanalysis* 10 (1929) 436–443.

——— "A contribution to the psychogenesis of manic-depressive states." 1935. *International Journal of Psychoanalysis* 16 (1945) 145–74.

——— "Notes on some schizoid mechanisms." *International Journal of Psycho-Analysis* 27 (1946) 99–110.

——— *Envy and Gratitude.* 1957; London: Vintage, 1997.

Koons, Jeff, and Norman Rosenthal. *Jeff Koons: Conversations with Norman Rosenthal.* London. New York: Thames & Hudson, 2014.

Latour, Bruno. *Reassembling the Social: An Introduction to Actor-Network-Theory.* Oxford: Oxford University Press, 2005.

Lehmann, John and Phillip Fry. "An Interview in Austin with John Lehmann." *Studies in the Novel* 3:1 (1971) 80–96.

Lethbridge, Lucy. *Servants: A Downstairs History of Britain from the Nineteenth Century to Modern Times*. New York: W. W. Norton & Company, 2013.

Lewis, Mindy. "Abhorring a Vacuum." In *Dirt: The Quirks, Habits and Passions of Keeping House*. Ed. Mindy Lewis. Berkeley, CA: Seal Press, 2009, pp. 141–50.

Lifshey, Earl. *The Housewares Story: A History of the American Housewares Industry*. Chicago: National Housewares Manufacturers Association, 1973.

Light, Alison. *Mrs Woolf and the Servants*. New York: Bloomsbury, 2008.

Lupton, Ellen. *Mechanical Brides: Women and Machines from Home to Office*. New York: Smithsonian Institute, 1991.

Maclaren-Ross, Julian. *Of Love and Hunger*. 1947; London: Penguin, 2002.

———— "Cosmopolitan Characters." Review of Aubry Menen, *The Backward Bride* and Roland Camberton, *Scamp*. *Times Literary Supplement* 2545 (10 November 1950) 705.

———— *Memoirs of the Forties*. 1965. In *Collected Memoirs*. London: Black Spring Press, 2001.

———— *Bitten by the Tarantula and Other Writing*. London: Black Spring Press, 2005.

———— *Selected Letters*. Ed. Paul Willetts. London: Black Spring Press, 2008.

Marchand, Roland. *Advertising the American Dream: Making Way for Modernity, 1920–1940*. Berkeley: University of California Press, 1985.

Marder, Michael. *Dust*. New York and London: Bloomsbury Academic, 2016.

Marling, Karal Ann. *As Seen on TV: The Visual Culture of Everyday Life in the 1950s*. Cambridge, MA: Harvard University Press, 1996.

Marx, Karl. *Capital*. 1867, Vol. 1, Section 4: "The fetishism of commodities and the secret thereof." https://www.marxists.org/archive/marx/works/1867-c1/ch01.htm#S4

Marx, Karl and Friedrich Engels, *Manifesto of the Communist Party*. 1848. Trans. Samuel Moore. https://www.marxists.org/archive/marx/works/download/pdf/Manifesto.pdf

May, Charles E. "Put Yourself in the Shoes of Raymond Carver." *Journal of the Short Story in English* 46 (2006) 31–42. https://journals.openedition.org/jsse/488.

McCully, Emily Arnold. "How's Your Vacuum Cleaner Working?" *The Massachusetts Review* 17:1 (1976) 23–43.

McKibben, Ross. *Classes and Cultures*. Oxford: Oxford University Press, 1998.

Meintjes, Helen. "'Washing Machines Make Lazy Women': Domestic Appliances and the Negotiation of Women's Propriety in Soweto." *Journal of Material Culture* 6:3 (2001) 345–363.

Miles, Barry. *Zappa*. New York: Grove Press, 2004.

Miller, Arthur. *Death of a Salesman*. 1949; New York: Viking, 1967.

Monti, Enrico. "*Il miglior fabbro?* On Gordon Lish's Editing of Raymond Carver's *What We Talk About When We Talk About Love.*" *Raymond Carver Review* 1 (2007) 53–72.

Morrison, Toni. *Paradise.* 1997; London: Vintage, 1999.

——— "The Work You Do, the Person You Are." *New Yorker* (June 5 & 12) 2017. https://www.newyorker.com/magazine/2017/06/05/toni-morrison-the-work-you-do-the-person-you-are

Morse, Donald E. "Sterile Men and Nuclear-Powered Vacuum Cleaners: The Atom Bomb and Atomic Energy in 1950s American Science Fiction." In Morse, Donald E. (ed) *Anatomy of Science Fiction.* Newcastle: Cambridge Scholars Press, 2006, pp. 83–9.

Neuhaus, Jessamyn. *Housework and Housewives in Modern American Advertising: Married to the Mop.* New York: Macmillan, 2011.

Nevett, T.R. *Advertising in Britain: A History.* London: Heinemann, 1982.

Nye, David N. *Electrifying America: Social Meanings of a New Technology.* Cambridge MA and London: MIT Press, 1990.

Oakley, Ann. *Housewife.* 1974; Harmondsworth: Penguin, 1990.

Oldenziel, Ruth. "Object/ions: Technology, Culture, and Gender." In Kingery, W. David (ed) *Learning from Things: Method and Theory of Material Culture Studies.* Washington, DC: Smithsonian Institution Press, 1995, pp. 55–69.

Olney, Martha L. *Buy Now, Pay Later: Advertising, credit, and consumer durables in the 1920s.* Chapel Hill: University of North Carolina Press, 1991.

Orwell, George. *Keep the Aspidistra Flying.* 1936; London: Penguin Classics, 2000.

———*The Road to Wigan Pier.* 1937; New York: Harcourt Brace and World, 1958.

——— *Coming Up for Air.* 1939; New York: Mariner Books, 1969.

Parr, Joy. "Modern Kitchen, Good Home, Strong Nation." *Technology and Culture* 434 (2004) 657–67.

Peavitt, Helen. *Refrigerator: The Story of Cool in the Kitchen.* London: Reaktion, 2017.

Peck, Winifred. *Housebound.* 1942; London: Persephone, 2007.

Pfaffenberger, Bryan. "Fetishised Objects and Humanised Nature: Towards an Anthropology of Technology." *Man NS* 23:2 (1988) 236–252.

Phillips, Sarah T. and Shane Hamilton. *The Kitchen Debate and Cold War Consumer Politics: A Brief History with Documents.* Boston, MA and New York: Bedford/St. Martin's, 2014.

Plain, Gill. *Women's Fiction of the Second World War: Gender, Power, and Resistance.* New York: St. Martin's Press, 1996.

——— *Literature of the 1940s: War, Postwar and "Peace."* Edinburgh: Edinburgh University Press, 2013.

Powell, Anthony. *Books Do Furnish a Room.* 1971. Book 10 of *A Dance to the Music of Time.* Chicago: University of Chicago Press, 2010.

Pratchett, Terry. *The Witch's Vacuum Cleaner and Other Stories*. London: Clarion Books, 2017.

Rees, Jonathan. *Refrigerator*. New York and London: Bloomsbury Academic, 2015.

Rose, Barbara. "Claes Oldenburg's Soft Machines." In Madoff, Steven Henry (ed) *Pop Art: A Critical History*. Berkeley: University of California Press, 1997, pp. 228–234.

Rosenberg, Karen. "A Low-Cost Show Re-inflates a Big Bag." *New York Times* (May 7, 2009) https://www.nytimes.com/2009/05/08/arts/design/08clae.html

Rosenthal, Bob. *Cleaning Up New York*. New York: The Little Bookroom, 2016.

Rosler, Martha. "Place, Position, Power, Politics." In *Decoys and Disruptions: Selected Writings, 1975–2001*. Cambridge, MA: MIT Press, 2004, pp. 349–378.

Rosner, Victoria. *Modernism and the Architecture of Private Life*. New York: Columbia University Press, 2005.

Russolo, Luigi. *The Art of Noise*. Trans. Robert Filliou. 1967; Ubu Classics, 2004. http://artype.de/Sammlung/pdf/russolo_noise.pdf

Sartre, Jean-Paul. *Being and Nothingness: An Essay on Phenomenological Ontology*. Trans. Hazel E. Barnes. 1943; New York: Philosophical Library, 1956.

Scaglione, Richard. *The Hungry Mean Washing Machine*. Independently published, 2022.

Scott, Peter. "The Twilight World of Interwar British Hire Purchase." *Past & Present* 177 (2002) 195-225.

———- "Managing Door-to-Door Sales of Vacuum Cleaners in Interwar Britain." *The Business History Review* 82:4 (2008) 761–788.

———- *The Market Makers: Creating Mass Markets for Consumer Durables in Inter-war Britain*. Oxford: Oxford University Press, 2017.

Scott, Peter and James Walker. "Power to the People: Working-class demand for household power in 1930s Britain." *Oxford Economic Papers* 63:4 (December 2011) 598–624.

Sebastian, Anna (a.k.a. Friedl Benedikt). *The Monster*. London: Jonathan Cape, 1944.

Shelton, Glen. *The Complete Guide to Door-to-Door Cold Knocking*. 2016. http://www.leadheroes.com/the-complete-guide-to-door-to-door-cold-knocking/

Sinclair, Iain. "Man in a Macintosh: Roland Camberton, the Great Invisible of English Fiction." Introduction to Camberton, Roland. *Scamp*, pp. 5–18.

Sklenicka, Carol. *Raymond Carver: A Writer's Life*. New York: Scribner, 2009.

Smith, Virginia. *Clean: A History of Personal Hygiene and Purity*. Oxford and New York: Oxford University Press, 2007.

Spears, Timothy B. *100 Years on the Road: The Traveling Salesman in American Culture*. New Haven and London: Yale University Press, 1995.

Steedman, Caroline. *Dust: The Archive and Cultural History*. New Brunswick, NJ: Rutgers University Press, 2001.

Strasser, Susan. *Never Done: A History of American Housework*. New York: Henry Holt, 2000.

Strong, Jeremy. *Fatbag, the Demon Vacuum Cleaner*. 1983; London: Puffin Books, 1993.

Sutherland, John. *Orwell's Nose: A Pathological Biography*. London; Reaktion, 2016.

Taber, Valerie. n.d. "The Symbolism and Iconography of Kerry James Marshall's 'Silence is Golden.'" https://scalar.chapman.edu/scalar/ah-329-black-subjects-in-white-art-history-fall-2020-compendium/essays

Taylor, Avram. "'Funny Money', Hidden Charges and Repossession: Working-class Experiences of Consumption and Credit in the Inter-war Years." In Benson and Ugolini (eds) *Cultures of Selling*, pp. 153–82.

Tratner, Michael. *Deficits and Desires: Economics and Sexuality in Twentieth-Century Literature*. Stanford, CA: Stanford University Press, 2001.

Usborne, Simon. "Sucks to be him! How Henry the vacuum cleaner became an accidental design icon." *The Guardian Weekend* (24 July 2021) 21–26. https://www.theguardian.com/lifeandstyle/2021/jul/24/how-henry-vacuum-cleaner-became-accidental-design-icon.

Varèse, Edgard. "The Liberation of Sound." Ed. Chou Wen-chung. *Perspectives of New Music* 5:1 (1966) 11–19.

Veltman, Andrea. "The Sisyphean Torture of Housework: Simone de Beauvoir and the Inequitable Divisions of Domestic Work in Marriage." *Hypatia* 19:3 (2004) 121–143.

Virilio, Paul. *Politics of the Very Worst*. New York: Semiotexte, 1999.

Warner, Sylvia Townsend. "'Modern Witches' – Episode Two," first published in *Eve* 18 (August 1926), *The Sylvia Townsend Warner Society Newsletter* 10 (2005) n.p.

Watson, Ben. "Frank Zappa's Legacy: Just Another Hoover?" *Circuit* 14:3 (2004) 33–44. https://doi.org/10.7202/902325ar.

Waugh, Evelyn. *Vile Bodies*. 1930; London: Penguin, 2000.

Willetts, Paul. *Fear and Loathing in Fitzrovia: The Bizarre Life of Writer, Actor, Soho Dandy Julian Maclaren-Ross*. Stockport: Dewi Lewis Publishing, 2003.

———— Afterword to the German edition of Maclaren-Ross, Julian. *Of Love and Hunger*. https://www.paulwilletts.com/2532807-of-love-and-hunger

Williams, Raymond. "The Realism of Arthur Miller." *Critical Quarterly* 1:2 (1959) 140–149.

Williams, William Carlos. "The Red Wheelbarrow." *Spring and All* XXII. 1923. *The Collected Poems of William Carlos Williams*, Vol. 1 1909-1939. Ed. A. Walton Litz and Christopher MacGowan. Manchester: Carcanet, 2000, p. 224.

Wilson, Mary. *The Labors of Modernism: Domesticity, Servants, and Authorship in Modernist Fiction*. Farnham, Surrey: Ashgate, 2013.

Winner, Langdon. *The Whale and the Reactor: A Search for Limits in an Age of High Technology.* 1986; Chicago: University of Chicago Press, 2020.

Woolf, Virginia. *A Room of One's Own.* 1929. Ed. Mark Hussey. New York: Mariner Books, 2005.

Zappa, Frank. *Hot Rats.* Album. 1969.

———, *Chunga's Revenge.* Album. 1970

———, "Edgard Varèse: The Idol of My Youth." *Stereo Review* (1971) 61–62. http://rchrd.com/mfom/zappa-varese.html

———, *Joe's Garage.* Album. 1979/1987.

———, Boulez Conducts Zappa*: The Perfect Stranger.* Album. 1983.

FILMS CITED

200 Motels. 1971. Dir. Frank Zappa and Tony Palmer. Murakami-Wolf-Swenson Bizarre Productions.

The Brave Little Toaster. 1987. Dir. Jerry Rees. Hyperion Pictures; The Kushner-Locke Company.

Glass Bottom Boat. 1966. Dir. Fred Tashlin. Metro Goldwyn Mayer.

The Green Man. 1956. Dir. Robert Day. Grenadier Films Ltd.

Our Man in Havana. 1959. Dir. Carol Reed. Columbia Pictures.

The President's Analyst. 1967. Dir. Theodore J. Flicker. Paramount.

Super Sucker (a.k.a. *Daft as a Brush*). 2002. Dir. Jack Daniels. Purple Rose Films.

Index[1]

[1] Note: Page numbers followed by 'n' refer to notes.

© The Author(s), under exclusive license to Springer Nature
Switzerland AG 2024
M. Ellmann, *The Vacuum Cleaner*, Material Modernisms,
https://doi.org/10.1007/978-3-031-56666-0

GPSR Compliance

The European Union's (EU) General Product Safety Regulation (GPSR) is a set of rules that requires consumer products to be safe and our obligations to ensure this.

If you have any concerns about our products, you can contact us on ProductSafety@springernature.com

In case Publisher is established outside the EU, the EU authorized representative is:

Springer Nature Customer Service Center GmbH
Europaplatz 3
69115 Heidelberg, Germany

The manufacturer's authorised representative in the EU is Springer
Nature Customer Service Centre GmbH, Europaplatz 3, 69115 Heidelberg,
Germany. If you have any concerns regarding our products, please
contact ProductSafety@springernature.com

Printed and bound by CPI Group (UK) Ltd, Croydon, CR0 4YY
24/04/2026
02096359-0004